D0915674

A
White Male
Running

By the same author:

Darling Corey's Dead

3 3503 00065 1301

A
White Male
Running

Martha G. Webb

State Library OF Ohio

SEO Library Center
40780 SR 821 * Caldwell, OH 43724

Walker and Company
New York

Copyright © 1985 by Martha G. Webb

All rights reserved. No part of this book may be
reproduced or transmitted in any form or by any
means, electronic or mechanical, including photocopying,
recording, or by any information storage and retrieval
system, without permission in writing from the Publisher.

All the characters and events portrayed in this story
are fictitious.

First published in the United States of America
in 1985 by the Walker Publishing Company, Inc.

Library of Congress Cataloging in Publication Data

Webb, Martha G.
    A white male running.

      I. Title.
PS3573.E196W48   1985   813'.54   85-630
ISBN 0-8027-5611-5

Book Design by Teresa M. Carboni

Printed in the United States of America

10 9 8 7 6 5 4 3 2 1

85-32218

In memoriam: Major Clinton "Doc" Luther,
Albany Police Department, Albany, Georgia

"I've got one running."

"Ten-four, North Car, you say
you've got one on the ground?"

"That's affirmative. I've got
a white male running north in the
alley from this location."

—Police radio conversation

PROLOGUE

THE DELIVERY BOY was whistling as he walked up the steps and swung the door open. Miss Libby was sometimes entertaining clients when he came, and he had instructions just to leave the groceries on the table. She'd pay the store later. She always did; she was a good customer, and of course he wasn't supposed to know about those clanking bottles at the bottom of the box that didn't come from Shelton's Grocery. At least, not officially.

He put the box down and glanced curiously into the next room, wondering what that rhythmic sound was. It didn't sound like what he usually heard. And then he saw.

The man was beating Miss Libby around the head with his cane. Miss Libby's head was all bloody, and she was hanging limp from the hand that he was clutching. There wasn't a sound in the room, except the noise of the cane and the man's breath.

The boy stared, terrified, and thought of running, then put the thought out of his mind. Mama always said *never* to run if you were right. But he couldn't fight that man, not a man that big, that was certain. Then the boy remembered a scene from a movie. The hero was small and the villain was big. The hero stopped the villain from beating a woman by putting a knife to his throat from behind and yelling.

The boy had a knife on his belt for cutting open boxes at the store. He was sure the man hadn't noticed him yet. He whipped the knife out and came in through the doorway. Just as he slid the knife around the man's neck the man jumped forward, Miss Libby slipping from his hand, and the boy felt the knife tear into the man's throat.

Looking at Miss Libby as she slid to the floor, the boy knew she had to be dead. The man whirled, the knife falling with a clatter to the floor beside Miss Libby's arm. His mouth was open but no sound was coming out. There was blood pouring down the front of his shirt, and the boy's horrified eyes registered the length of the cut around the base of his neck. How could so short a knife—but there wasn't time to think. The man was reaching for him.

He jumped back, and the man slipped in the blood on the floor and fell heavily. The boy turned and ran.

Two blocks away he remembered that, because the knife was a birthday present, his uncle had spent laborious hours carving the boy's name on its bone handle. Shuddering, he retraced his steps and picked up the bone-handled knife he found lying in the blood on the floor. He washed the blood off his hands and the knife in Miss Libby's wash basin. Then he fled again.

On his way home, he hurled the knife into a construction pit.

GRISLY MURDER IN VICE DISTRICT:
POLICE SEEK CLUES IN GHASTLY CRIME

The boy didn't dare read past the headlines.
The year was 1941, and the boy was twelve years old.

8

I

HER NAME WAS Rosemary. She had short brown hair and a pixie face. She was fourteen, and she would never learn to read. She was sitting on the porch swing rocking her doll and reflecting, dreamily, on people she knew.

Sometimes a man named Smoky came to visit her. He told Rosemary she was pretty like his mother. He had a little boy with pretty red hair. Rosemary liked to see people with pretty hair. Smoky had a gun and handcuffs on his belt. They were shiny, and sometimes he let Rosemary play with the handcuffs. But he said little girls mustn't touch guns.

"Pretty," Rosemary said to her doll. That was a word she could say. And she could say shiny. And she could say nice. She could think more things than she could say. But her mouth couldn't learn how to shape for the words to come out. Most people couldn't understand her.

Melissa could always understand her. Melissa was a blond lady. Her hair wasn't as pretty as Smoky's little boy's, but it was very long. Rosemary wasn't allowed to have long hair because it got all tangled up. She liked to play with Melissa's hair. Most people wouldn't let Rosemary play with their hair, but Melissa always did.

When Rosemary's parents went away at night Melissa stayed there. Melissa said she was going to be a doctor. Rosemary couldn't see how Melissa could be a doctor. Melissa was Melissa. The doctor was named Mack.

One day Melissa brought somebody named Tommy to visit Rosemary. Tommy had a gun, too. His hair was brown and curly like Rosemary's and almost as long as

9

Melissa's. His gun wasn't shiny, and he didn't have any handcuffs for Rosemary to play with. He wouldn't let Rosemary play with his hair, either. Rosemary guessed little girls made him nervous.

Sometimes another man came to visit Rosemary. He was very tall, and Rosemary didn't like the way his hair looked, the way he smelled, or the games he played. But he gave her candy and ice cream if she would play his games.

It was a violet-skied April twilight and Rosemary was two months pregnant. In four hours Rosemary would be dead.

The chief was right, of course.

A forty-seven person police department couldn't afford to have two people assigned just to narcotics, and as long as Tommy Inman was working undercover he clearly couldn't work on anything *but* narcotics.

Which meant Tommy couldn't work on keeping track of all the myriad pieces of information coming in from numbered snitches, concerned citizens and a dozen other sources, and piecing them all together into a coherent picture. He couldn't take out and serve search warrants and arrest warrants; he couldn't drive evidence to Garland to the state lab, or testify in court. All that was still on Smoky O'Donnell, who had worked intelligence and narcotics by himself for a year, even though now he was back catching calls in the detective bureau just like everybody else.

Smoky—Lieutenant Liam O'Donnell—was feeling very sorry for himself.

He guessed it was partly frustration. The baby was due any day now, and at the doctor's insistence (because Audra had started the pregnancy so run-down from last winter's flu) the boy was staying at his grandmother's house. Smoky could see that Audra couldn't really cope with him right now, and of course with his chaotic schedule he couldn't do much, but he didn't like it all the same. He also didn't like having Audra feeling so tired, the way she always did now, or having her (tell yourself the truth, anyway, he scolded himself) off limits to him.

And now all this had to come up.

As politicians went, he guessed he liked Dave Barnett as well as he did any politician. But April seemed such an odd time to be announcing a candidacy. It just wasn't convenient.

People rarely consult the convenience of cops, though, which was why Smoky O'Donnell wound up spending Tuesday evening in the Grand Ballroom of the Lee Hotel, not really so grand a ballroom. It had housed a few proms, perhaps, but its usual function was that of a meeting room for the Rotary, the Kiwanis, the Lions, and the Exchange Club, each of which had one Tuesday luncheon a month.

Now the battered golden oak podium was covered with the inevitable red, white, and blue crepe paper, as people gathered to hear an official announcement of the already-known fact that David Barnett was running for Texas State Senator. The barely begun term of office had been held by Hank Rogers, who had retired after suffering two strokes in three months.

It probably would get to be an interesting race. Karl Smithers had already announced he was running. Smithers had the post before Rogers, who had not run for reelection because he wanted to stay home and mind his oil wells. The oil wells proved to be less profitable in his own hands than in those of his chairman of the board, so he decided it might be advisable to return to politics. He had expected to be unopposed.

And he was, until Dave Barnett entered the race. Dave's candidacy made him, in Mound County at least, a political anomaly—almost, one might be tempted to say, a dark horse candidate.

Smoky was glad he hadn't made that joke aloud because the reason the chief had found it necessary to have a detective lieutenant on hand when Dave Barnett announced his candidacy was that Dave Barnett was black. The chief was afraid he might be needing a little protection.

That seemed an odd thought in a town less than twenty miles northeast of Dallas, a town that was really little more than a bedroom community. But going northeast of Dallas meant leaving its cosmopolitan world behind and driving into the Old South; the towns in the northeast corner of Texas, such as Marshall and Jefferson, can scarcely be distinguished from similar-sized towns in Georgia and Alabama.

Of course, that doesn't hold true in all the bedroom communities. Plano, for instance, grew from five thousand to eighty-five thousand people in the last twenty years and totally lost its small-town character in the process. But Farmer's Mound, just a little farther north and east, has only gone from thirty-five thousand to forty thousand in the same twenty years, and the only change has been that many of its people now commute to offices instead of walking out the door to farm their lands.

The mound that gave the town its name has been thoroughly examined by archaeologists and proclaimed a natural hill and not an Indian Mound at all, but in general the people at Farmer's Mound don't believe the archaeologists. Farmer's Mound still looks like a little town in Alabama, complete with red brick streets and a Confederate statue on the courthouse lawn. And it has the same kind of problems, even if its schools have been integrated for fifteen years.

All the same, the evening had gone smoothly enough. Smoky wasn't drinking, being officially on duty, but everybody else was. The group was, for Farmer's Mound, surprisingly mixed, with black and white men and women mingling quite happily. There was a knot of reporters mostly—but not all—black from Dallas and Fort Worth papers, clustered in one corner; Smoky guessed they'd stay till the ballroom was deserted. One local newspaperman was there—Matt Carson, who covered political news for the Farmer's Mound *News Messenger*. He'd refused to take Barnett seriously at first, but by the time Barnett was in his second term on the city council Carson had to admit he seemed to know what he was doing.

And being Matthew Carson, he had done so quite publicly, in a lengthy editorial.

The speeches were over now, and Barnett was moving through the crowd, drinking only rarely from the Scotch glass in his hand and first-naming everybody with the practiced ease of a long-time politician. He stopped in front of Smoky. "You're not drinking tonight?"

"Afraid I'm on duty," Smoky said.

"When do you get off duty?"

"When you get home safely."

"Oh, is that the way of it?" Barnett's face suddenly didn't look like a politician's at all. "I didn't ask for that."

"I know you didn't. The chief thought it might be advisable."

"Did you get drafted for it," Barnett asked, "or did the chief ask for volunteers?"

"It was a draft. But as you well know, I'm familiar with most of the bad asses in town. It was logical."

"You are at that," Barnett agreed. "Black and white ones both. Which did he expect trouble from?"

"Neither," Smoky said. "It was just a precaution, that's all. Do you resent my being here? I don't mind it. I wouldn't want you to get hurt, but I don't expect trouble."

"Neither do I. But no, I don't resent you being here—not you, anyhow. I just . . . resent having anybody feel it's necessary." He looked, unseeing, down at his glass. "No, that's not true either. What I resent is the fact that it is necessary. It ought not to be. Not now. Twenty years ago, maybe. But not now." He looked back up, eyes steady on Smoky, and for a moment Smoky felt immense pity for

13

this quiet, reasonable man trapped in a situation that definitely was not of his making.

But only for a moment, because the situation was infinitely better than it had been forty years ago, and had the potential to go on getting better, as long as the future stayed in the hands of reasonable people. Like David Barnett.

He wondered why Barnett was running for office from Farmer's Mound, why he hadn't moved over to Dallas where he'd have a real chance. But one of the reporters had asked that tonight, and Barnett had answered, "Because this is my home. I live here. My law office is in Dallas, but I've always lived in Farmer's Mound. And I *do* have a chance to win from here. If I didn't I wouldn't be running."

Someone came over, whispered in Barnett's ear from behind cupped hands. Barnett nodded. "Excuse me," he said to Smoky.

He went to the closest phone, which was just behind the podium, and only Smoky heard him say, softly, "Then why don't you give them to Cynthia? I'm sure she'd be amused." He listened and Smoky, who had turned to watch him, saw flashing anger. "If that's what you think, then why don't you find it, bastard? But forget trying to invent one. You're damned unconvincing." He hung up, hard.

Smoky, who had been quietly edging toward him, said, "Trouble?"

The angry eyes looked past Smoky for a moment and then focussed back on him. "Not really. But I do think I'd better have a private talk with you." He looked across the room. "Matt!"

Carson turned, greying brown hair down in front of his eyes as usual, and said, "Yeah?"

The reporters surged in that direction. "Not all of you," Barnett said. "I'm not holding a news conference for

God's sake; I just did that. I want to talk to Matt for a few minutes."

In a small office off the ballroom, Barnett faced the reporter and the cop. "That phone call I just got," he said. "It's going to get worse, and you two need to know about it."

"Go on," Smoky said softly, as Barnett lapsed into silence, looking down at his hands.

"It's a nut," Barnett said. "I mean, the guy's got to be some kind of squirrel. He's been calling and writing me for months, and I'm sure it's the same guy because he's cross-referenced calls and letters. He wanted to be sure I knew they were all from him. For a while it was just general bad-mouthing, that kind of thing, and then he started trying to blackmail me. And all of it he makes up. One time—this one the postal inspector's working on—he had some obscene photos. You know, the composite kind."

"I saw them," Smoky said.

Barnett looked startled. "You did?"

"When Jerry was checking them for prints," Smoky said. "The postal inspector thought it might be somebody in our files. You could tell they were fakes, if you looked hard. But they were good." He grinned. "All right. I mean they were skillfully done. The guy's a photographer or knows one."

"That was the thing that worried me most," Barnett said. "Most of his other stuff was really stupid. This phone call, it was supposed to be some letters I'd written some whore. I told him—well, you heard what I told him."

"And he said?" Matt asked softly. "I heard your end of the conversation, too."

"He said—it was bad-mouthing, mostly. But he said he knew there was really something that could destroy me and he could prove it." He turned the squat plastic tumbler around on the table, staring at the water-beads circling and sliding. As Barnett continued carefully, Smoky, watching his hands, saw creased black knuckles taut with the effort to appear relaxed. "Whatever he comes up with, I don't pay him. If I ever did, once, I'd be in his pocket the rest of my life. So if something about me comes to either one of you, would you check with me before you do anything else?"

"I'd do that anyway," Carson said. "Now. Four years ago, no, I'd have asked everywhere else before I asked you. But not now."

"I'd ask you, if something like that happened," Smoky said, "but it would help me to find him if you'd give me some more information."

"Don't bother to try to find him," Barnett said. "I don't think it's worth the trouble. I think if he was going to use any of this he already would have. It's just that it bothers Cynthia, and I had promised her if he contacted me again I'd let the police and the news people know about it. Sub rosa, so to speak. You know."

But Smoky, watching his eyes, watching his hands, knew he was looking at a very frightened man. And I need to know, he thought, why you're so scared.

But you don't argue with a politician, and you especially don't argue with David Barnett. Smoky went back to the ballroom, inconspicuous to anyone who didn't know him, a small slender man with dark blond hair beginning to grey at the temples. With his back to the wall, he kept guarded grey eyes on the crowd and sipped listlessly on a ginger ale until it got late enough that he could go home to Audra.

Unlike Smoky, Tommy Inman did not consider himself to be on duty. In oil-streaked blue jeans and tee-shirt, with his long brown hair held carelessly back out of his eyes with a leather shoestring, he was sitting on the concrete floor of Hatfield's Chopper Shop. He and Buck Walters were working on Buck's bike. Buck had skinned some chrome pretty bad and they were trying to decide if they could polish it back out or if they'd have to replace it.

Right now, Tommy and Buck were friends. They had been friends a long time, and Buck hadn't much cared when Tommy put out his last reefer two years ago and never lit another. People do change their minds about that sort of thing. But Buck hadn't known that a year later Tommy went through the Regional Police Academy in Grand Prairie. And Buck didn't know about the work Tommy was doing now.

Tommy didn't figure the friendship would survive the day Buck found out. But he liked Buck anyway, and he'd enjoy the friendship while it lasted. Maybe he wouldn't miss Buck much, when it was over. Because then he could marry Melissa, Melissa who was a cop's daughter, Melissa who couldn't be seen with him in public as long as he was working undercover—Melissa who had the 6 P.M. to 2 A.M. shift tonight at the hospital, which was why Tommy was working on a motorcycle tonight.

"This just looks like chickenshit," Buck said mournfully, regarding the seventy-five dollars' worth of chrome. What really hurt was, he hadn't messed it up himself. He'd had to go on a detour, around a road under construction, and he'd been riding as soft as a kitten to keep that gravel still. But he'd been passed by the proverbial beaver in a Camaro, and the gravel shooting up from her rear wheels had liberally sprayed both him and his bike. He'd mend, but that chrome—

Tommy, sitting Indian-style, dropped his elbows down on his knees, one dirty hand in his hair, and cocked his head over sideways. "It just ain't gonna polish out, Buck."

Eddie Reno wandered in through the shop door, which was open to the soft spring night. "You guys are workin' late."

"Yeah," said Tommy. Eddie Reno was one dude he emphatically didn't like. Although Tommy's days as a street cop were yet to come, he was well on his way to developing street cop instincts. And the cop in him said, this bastard's no good.

Eddie, oblivious to Tommy's opinion of him, squatted down beside them. "You sure done you a job on that one, Buck," he muttered. "You sure did."

"Yeah," Buck said. He didn't like Eddie either. Tommy didn't know why. Maybe he ought to find out.

"Hey, look," Eddie said, "how long are you guys going to stay here?"

"Till we get through," Buck grunted. Like several other bikers, he had an agreement with Joe Hatfield. The bikers were allowed to use the shop area all they wanted to after hours, provided they paid for the parts they used, cleaned up after themselves, and made sure the place didn't get burglarized.

"Why do you want to know?" Tommy asked.

"Cause I need some help and I thought maybe you dudes would help me."

"Help you do what?"

"Help me get some stuff out of a house."

"I ain't no burglar." Buck was lying on his back now, one knee bent, trying to look at the underside of his fender.

"It ain't like a burglar. The lady the stuff belongs to, she's, well, she's dead, is what she is."

"How'd she get dead?" Tommy asked.

"She—well, look, if you don't want to help me—" Eddie was acting increasingly nervous.

"I ain't *said* I don't want to help you," Tommy said. "I just want to know what I'm getting into. Now don't that make sense?"

Eddie gulped. "Look," he said, "I don't know how she got dead, see? I'm just doing a guy a favor. This guy, he lives way out the other side of town, and he told me this lady just up and died in his house and he had got rid of the body because it would have been too hard to explain what she was doing in his house, and he knew how to make it look like she'd left town, only he just wanted somebody to get her stuff out of her house and he didn't want to go over there himself. You talk about stuff making sense, don't *that* make sense?"

"I guess," Tommy said grudgingly.

"But I went over there and looked," Eddie went on, "and some of the stuff he wanted moved weighs a lot, there was a big old chifforobe and I can't move it by myself. I got a pickup truck and all that but I just need somebody to help me move stuff, and he said he'd pay me real good if we just go clean the place up and move her stuff out. That chifforobe is the only piece of the furniture that's hers. I tell you what, I give each of you guys fifty dollars if you help me. Ain't that a simple job?"

"Yeah, pretty simple," Tommy said, looking at Eddie keenly. His mind was racing. What was the best thing for him to do? This situation could wind up blowing hell out of his cover, but he had to figure something out. If he said no, I won't help you, Eddie would just go find somebody else to do the work. And if he said yes, I'll help you, and then went right over there and set to work, well, in the first place he'd be an accessory, and in the second place, he'd be messing the crime scene up something awful. He knew not to do that.

"Look here, Buck," Tommy said, "if it's true she didn't die in the house we can't get in too much trouble, and it would be easy money. Let's just go over there and see how much work Eddie's talking about."

"I don't like that kind of stuff," Buck said, "but—" He looked at the chrome. "Them parts don't come free. Okay, Eddie. You got your truck with you?"

Probably, Tommy thought, cops all over town automatically took note in their minds when and where they saw this truck, Eddie's reputation being quite well known. But nobody stopped them on the ten-minute trip across town; in fact, they didn't even see a police car.

There wasn't much doubt, Tommy thought inside the house, that the woman—whoever she was—had died right here. There wasn't too much blood, but it doesn't always take much blood. The way things were thrown about—and the smell in the place—this guy that Eddie was talking about was a fool, whoever he was, if he figured by moving the victim's personal property out he could hide what had happened here. "Have you started doing anything yet?" Tommy asked, standing about four feet inside the front door, with Buck silent beside him.

"Not yet," Eddie said from behind him.

Tommy didn't figure he had. Eddie was notoriously good at getting other people to do his dirty work for him.

"Well, here's my ideas about this," Tommy said. "Let's just leave it for tonight. If we start trying to move stuff out of here right now what's going to happen is, the pigs will come along and spot us and put a burglary rap on us, and you know there ain't no way we can prove it ain't burglary." Because, he thought, burglary is exactly what it is—or at least one of the things it is. "So let's wait till morning and bring the truck up to the front door, all nice and open, and when the cops come and ask what we're doing, we'll tell them the lady sent us to get her stuff and store it for her. That sound all right to you?" Sometime tonight, he thought, he'd get to a phone. By the time he and Eddie and Buck could get to the apartment in the morning, police would already be here.

"That sounds fine," Eddie said enthusiastically. "Well, then, let's get out of here for now. I'll run you guys back out to Hatfield's and go get my bike and meet you later at the Sonic, okay? I got me—hey, I got me some good grass, you guys want a reefer I'll give you one, okay?" He was sounding very relieved.

"Okay," Buck said. "I ain't had none in a while."

And Tommy could never quite figure out, later, just what had happened to make the evening turn out as it did. They had stayed at the Sonic for a while, until it closed at eleven, and then gone over to the Safeway parking lot to continue talking. Somehow, at some point, Tommy must have said the wrong thing, although he could never figure out what the wrong thing he said was. They had been talking about how the man had disposed of the body of the woman, and Eddie had said she was in a car somewheres, and Tommy wondered where the car was and nobody knew, and then they were talking about the grass Eddie had gotten hold of. It was good grass, the kind that's called Acapulco Gold and is so hard to get ahold of nowadays, and Buck had lit his up and Tommy had stuck his in his shirt pocket and said, "Later. I'll smoke it later," and then somehow things had gotten quiet.

Real quiet.

"An abortion? My God, she died of a botched *abortion*? Who in Christ's name—?" It was a mixture of grief and rage, and it would be a few more minutes before Smoky could get back to thinking like a cop. He had cared a lot about Rosemary.

It was after midnight. Captain Simons had called him out to the hospital at eleven-thirty, just after he'd gotten home from the political thing. Simons was violently angry and very concerned about a slim blond nurse, who happened to be his daughter Melissa.

But Melissa, who was paying her way through school by being a part-time LVN assigned to the emergency room, was holding up; she was white-faced but not weeping yet, working hard at not weeping because she knew if she started crying she'd ask for Tommy and she couldn't have Tommy because he was out somewhere in the night on a black and chrome Harley buying heroin.

But as the doctor stood in the hall, trying to explain to the police (and to Melissa, because she wouldn't go away) what had happened to Rosemary, Tommy came into the emergency room with his helmet in his hand. He walked past through the receiving area and through the swinging door and on into the hall and put the helmet down on a gurney and said, very quietly and very distinctly, "Somebody, I need some help."

Three cops and a doctor and a nurse and Melissa turned to look at him, and as Melissa raised her arms toward him he reached for her and said, "Please don't scream, Lissa, I've got a headache." Then his knees started to buckle and Smoky, beside him by that time, got an arm around him. Together Smoky and Melissa got him lying down.

"It's not really that bad," he was trying to say. "And I did really want to get a haircut and now I guess I can get a haircut tomorrow." He took a deep breath. "I know I look sort of awful but it's really not that bad, honest."

At a glance Smoky could tell he'd been stomped rather thoroughly, but he was inclined to agree that the injuries weren't especially serious. "I'm sorry, son," he said. "How did it happen?"

"I don't know," Tommy said, and turned on his side on the narrow gurney, drawing his knees up. With his face away from Smoky and one hand on Melissa's waist, he said, "I don't know what gave me away but something did. I ain't undercover no more." He turned on his back again. "What's going on here? You weren't all waiting up for me."

"Rosemary's dead," Melissa said, one hand raised to hide her face now. "Tommy, Rosemary's dead."

"Rose—you mean that girl you babysit? Rosemary? How can Rosemary be dead? What happened to her?" Cautiously, he sat back up.

Cardew told him what happened to Rosemary. Tommy gently pushed away the nurse who was washing his face and reached for Melissa. "Cry," he told her, "cry, Lissa. . . . For God's sake," he appealed to the nurse, "isn't there something you can give her to let her cry?"

"I'll be okay," Melissa choked, "and you just lay back down."

"You'll both be okay," the doctor said in the doorway. "Melissa, sit down before you fall down. You're off duty right now. I've got Gloria coming in to finish your shift. Inman, I want you X-rayed before I do anything about you. Do you think you can hold off on medication till then?"

"It's not that bad," Tommy said patiently. "Yes, I can wait. I'm okay."

"Tommy," Smoky said, "while we're waiting for them to get the X-rays set up, I want you to tell me what happened."

Curled on his side again, Tommy closed his eyes. "Okay," he said. "I don't—like I said, I don't know what gave me away. I said something wrong and I don't know what—it was probably about my keeping that grass in my pocket instead of smoking it. Get it, would you, it's in my shirt pocket."

He didn't know what he'd said wrong, something—something had slipped out the wrong way and suddenly there was dead silence, at midnight, in the Safeway parking lot, where just a moment before nine people had been all trying to talk at once. And then someone said, not with suspicion but with dead-cold certainty, "You're a snitch. This time I'm sure. You're a Goddamn snitch for Smoky O'Donnell."

"Who, *me*?" Tommy said lightly, as he'd said a time or two before. But this time, he already knew the denial would do no good.

Under the streetlight he could see the dull gleam of a bicycle chain in somebody's hand. He tried to reach for his pistol but it was gone already, he felt it leave his pocket as his hand went toward it. He tried to get to his bike but the way was blocked. If he'd kept his helmet on—but he hadn't, it was twenty impassable yards from him, sitting on his bike.

He couldn't fight that many, and something caught his ankle and he went down. Then he knew only one thing to do—that was use his arms (and be thankful he'd put the jacket on) to shield his head and face from the chains, but then that left no way to defend the rest of his body from the heavy-toed boots that were methodically kicking at him. It was hard to get his breath; dimly he could hear his own voice gasping, choking, incoherently crying out only in pain, with no hope whatever of mercy.

Finally, after an eternity that really couldn't have been over two or three minutes, he heard someone say sharply, "Stop it. Right now."

And unbelievably, it stopped. Tommy, still curled on the asphalt surface of the parking lot trying to get his breath, dared not to believe it was over. It would start again. They wouldn't let him off this easy. Then someone caught him by the hair and jerked his head up, and he was looking dizzily into the hard-set face of Buck Walters.

"The truth, this time," Buck told him grimly. "You aren't just a snitch, are you?"

"No," Tommy said.

"Then tell 'em, tell 'em all, because now I know."

And it was over. It wouldn't do any good to lie anymore, and anyhow, Tommy wanted to tell the truth. He'd been wanting to, and maybe that was partly what gave him away. "I'm a cop," he said, and expected those three words to be the last he would ever say. But they weren't, and so he said them again. "I'm a cop. I'm a cop." And almost, despite the pain and the fear, he enjoyed their looks of dismay. "Yeah," he said, "sure, you can stomp me, but you can't stop it. Not now. All the nice evidence, it's all up in Smoky's office, all the stuff I bought from you, and all about your suppliers and all about your stashes and all I know about all of you. If you kill me, Smoky'll just get somebody up here from the

24

Metro intelligence squad, or even DEA, to finish the job I started. And now what do you plan to do about it?''

He guessed it was an answer, when he saw his own gun with the muzzle pointed toward his head. But Buck grabbed the gun. "No," he said, "my God, you damn fool, didn't you hear him say he's got all our names? They'd know just where to look. And they waste cop-killers in this state.''

"Then what—"

"Just listen, would you?" Buck faced Tommy. "All right, you've got us all—on drugs. But ain't none of us going to get much time for drugs. I'll make a deal with you.''

"What kind of deal?''

Buck spat on the asphalt. "You've made your last buy. I think you know what we think of you. If you'll forget who stomped you, we'll let you stay alive.''

And it wasn't too long ago that Tommy Inman had been on Buck's side of the badge. That sounded to him like a fair deal. "I'll agree to that.''

An angry voice. "Buck, how do we know he won't double-cross us? He's Goddamn well been doing it for a year.''

"You don't know," Tommy said, "just like I don't know you won't pull that trigger. But I give you my word and on that I'll keep it.''

He held his breath as Buck said, "If we kill him we're gone to Huntsville, all of us who don't fry, with what he's already turned in on us. We've got to let him go.''

"I don't want to be caught with his gun.''

"Then give it back to me," Tommy said.

"No way. I'll give it to Buck. He can give it back to you if he wants to.''

There were motor sounds.Tommy looked up again. He was alone with Buck Walters. "Here's your gun," Buck said.

"Thanks," said Tommy.

"I don't want to be no damn cop-killer," Buck said. "I

couldn't stop 'em from kicking you. There wasn't no use trying to stop 'em till they'd worked off some of the mad."

Tommy put the gun back in his pocket. "I know that," he said.

"Kicked you some myself," Buck added thoughtfully.

"Saw your boot," Tommy replied.

"Are you going to rat on us?"

"No," Tommy said. As he reached his bike, he turned. Buck was watching him, silently, eyes narrowed under the streetlight. "Buck," he said, "don't go back to that house tomorrow."

Then he had gone to the hospital, to walk in and ask for help.

"You aren't going to tell me who did it?" asked Smoky.

"No. And don't blame Buck. I'm not hurt."

"No, guess you aren't," Smoky agreed, eyeing Tommy coolly with experience that came from long before he was a cop, when he was a slum kid running the back streets of East Dallas. There were cuts and bruises, and Tommy would not forget it immediately, but there was no permanent harm.

"I'm not even really mad at them," Tommy added. "I can understand why they did it. I got off light, considering. But listen, about Buck. He did kick me once. I did recognize his boot. There was another guy who had on cowboy boots, you know, with real sharp toes, and he was aiming—God, it would've hurt, but Buck got there first, with round-toed boots, and—and the other guy hit the back of Buck's boot, which was what Buck meant to happen. And then he kept them from killing me. I won't ever forget that."

"I'm sure you won't," Smoky agreed, privately resolving Ham Walters would know it as soon as possible. Because Ham, that good deputy sheriff, had broken his heart over the wild doper his only son Buck had become. "Tommy," he added, "you'll be angry, later, at the others. Right now, you're glad to be alive. But tomorrow, you'll be hurting all over, and remembering crawling will burn you inside. There's one thing you've got to decide right now. One day you'll have the chance for revenge on the others, and you've got to know what you're going to do, because if you wait to decide then and act on impulse you may regret it. The one who hit you across the face with a chain, the one who kicked you where it hurt the most, you've caught them in the act of burglary, you've got them in your gun-sights. What are you going to do?"

"Recite a Miranda warning," Tommy said, "unless they resist arrest. I hear what you're asking. In a way I did make that promise under duress, but it was a promise and I'll keep it." He wiped oozing blood from his face with the back of his hand. "I only crawled literally, Smoky. And that doesn't matter much."

"You sound okay to me," Melissa said, trying to sound unconcerned. "If the doctor says the X-rays are all right will you take me home in my car? Because my daddy says he has to work all night, and I don't want to go home alone, and besides that you don't need to be trying to ride that motorcycle tonight."

"Yeah, sure, Melissa," he said, "only it may be kind of late. Smoky," he added, "one thing bothers me. I was just starting to get somewhere on one I was really interested in."

"Well, you can't catch 'em all," Smoky said. "You've accomplished a lot in the time you were on it. Let it die down for a while and then we'll follow that one up another way."

II

HE WAS MOVING stiffly with tape on three cracked ribs. His hair still wasn't Marine length, but now it was curling gently around his ears, with about a foot of it left on the floor of a barber shop fifteen minutes before. He was wearing blue jeans and motorcycle boots when he came into the detective bureau at ten o'clock. "I don't have a uniform," he announced. "And you have my badge in your desk drawer."

"Here," Smoky said, and pitched it to him. "Sorry," he added, as Tommy awkwardly recovered the passcase from the floor, "forgot you weren't bending so good. Don't you want to take a couple of days of sick leave?"

"No, I want to go to work," Tommy said. The blue .38 had moved from his jacket pocket to a basketweave holster strapped to a broad black belt. His face was clean, if somewhat cut and bruised, and Smoky, looking at him, had to suppress a grin. This wasn't the Tommy Inman he'd met a year ago, when he had to have an undercover man fast to clear a killing. This Tommy Inman was nearly up to the two hundred and twenty pounds he needed to fill out the big-boned six-foot-two frame. The eyes that then had been bored and defiant were now sparkling with lively enthusiasm. That Tommy Inman was a biker on a dead-end street. This Tommy Inman was a cop.

"Tom, I don't think we've got a uniform to fit you," Smoky told him. "We may have to keep you in the detective bureau until we can get a couple of uniforms made."

"I wouldn't mind that if the detective bureau

wouldn't," Tommy said cheerfully. "Besides, there's something real important I forgot to tell you last night. It was . . ."

"In a car?" Smoky repeated when Tommy finished. "What car? Where?"

"Well, that I don't know," Tommy said. "Eddie might know, if there was any way of making him tell."

"Let's try," Smoky proposed, standing up. "Chuck and Linn are working on Rosemary, so let's you and me just see what we can find out about this murder of yours."

"Eddie probably does know where the body is," Tommy repeated, "if we can just get him to tell us. He's not going to be too happy with me right now."

"Break out the violins," Smoky drawled. "Will Eddie be at home, do you think?"

"Well, if he had good sense, I'd figure he'd have run by now," Tommy said, "but being as he's Eddie, he's probably over trying to talk Buck into going to move that chifforobe."

"Then let's go see Buck."

On the way to the car, Tommy said slowly, "I'm not sure I want to see Buck."

"Why?"

"Because, of all the dopers in town, Buck's the only one that I care what he thinks of me."

Key in the ignition, Smoky paused. "You knew this day was coming, Tommy."

"I—yes. I did. But I didn't know Buck that well then." He grinned. "Don't worry, Smoke, I'm not going to back out now. I'm just saying it's going to be a little unpleasant."

"Then let's get it behind you instead of in front."

The brown Fury stopped in front of the little duplex where Buck Walters lived, and Smoky and Tommy got out. The front door opened, and Buck came onto the porch. "I figured I'd see you two this morning," he said. "Have you got a warrant?"

"A warrant for what?" Smoky asked blankly. "Tommy, is there something you haven't told me?"

"Uh-uh," Tommy said, his open hands extended well away from his body. "No warrants, Buck. That's the reason for an undercover. Smoky wasn't trying to get users. It's always easy to get them. He's after the dealers. And if you ever deal I don't know nothing about it."

"Then what are you here for?" Buck's eyes were still angry and confused, but his long rangy body visibly relaxed as he walked on down the stairs past his bike. "I didn't want to be arrested, you know. I got a—I got a wife and kid to look after, and Treesa, she can't hold down no job. But I figured, if you wanted to bust me, there wasn't no sense in trying to run. But if that ain't it, then what are you here for?"

"Information," Smoky said, watching him.

"Uh-uh. I ain't no snitch."

"Not that kind of information," Tommy said. "I got it myself, all you got access to. I just want to know if you've seen Eddie this morning. Because we really do have to find that body he was talking about, and if Eddie doesn't know where it is he knows who does know. Which would be a lot easier than going out and looking in every car in the county."

"No, I haven't seen him. He's stupid, but he ain't a running dumbass. He won't be going back to that house after last night. And she was killed there, at least from what I could tell."

"I noticed," Tommy said. "I sort of thought you did too. If—maybe I've got no business asking you anything, but if you hear anything more about that body, would you let me know?"

"I'll think about it." He turned and went back up on the porch, barefoot and shirtless, and then turned back around to look at them from across the yard. "Tommy," he said, "I don't like the kind of job you were doing. I damn well don't like it at all. But I'll have to give you credit for guts. I didn't figure you had it in you."

"Thanks," Tommy said, swinging open the door to the Fury. "See you around."

In the car, Smoky said, "Let's you and me go over and have a look at that house before we do any more work on hunting Eddie. We may want to get Jerry over there to start a crime scene on it, or we may just want to post a stakeout inside it for a while."

Texas in April is entering the spring flowers stage. The air is filled with the scent of redbud and dogwood blossoms, and the roadsides blaze with Indian paintbrush and Indian blanket and waves of bluebonnets. Usually it is cool in April. But today it was warm; Smoky figured it would be 85 degrees or higher by noon, which didn't speak too well for the probable condition of the missing body when they found it. That would be a smell no amount of wild flowers could mask.

The house was on Fourth Street. It wasn't much, as houses went. Smaller than a shot house, it had a grey stucco exterior, a very small kitchen, a very small bathroom, and another room which was living room, bedroom, dining room, and anything else anybody might want to use it for.

The one double bed was unmade, its only sheet half pulled off on the floor. There was blood on the sheet and on the mattress, and a bad smell hung over everything. Whatever happened in this room, it had happened a while ago.

Smoky walked around, not touching anything except door and drawer handles. "You say Eddie didn't bother anything?" As he spoke he opened the refrigerator door and then closed it rapidly.

"He says he didn't. I'm inclined to believe it." Tommy stood just inside the door, being careful not to disturb anything. Unlike Smoky, he wasn't opening doors or drawers.

Smoky, his hands in his pockets, walked into the bathroom. He came back out in a hurry. "God," he said. He took a deep breath at the front door and went back in again. He emerged looking grim. "We've got to find that body."

"What is it?" Tommy left the door to go look in the bathroom for himself. "Oh, my God!"

It was in the bathroom shower stall, and it was a rather large fetus to have been aborted—about five months, Smoky guessed, because curled as it was it was about eight inches long, and there were small evidences that it might have lived for maybe a couple of hours. The smell was partly coming from it and the rotting body tissues around it, and partly from the blood-soaked layers of newspaper it was lying on. No doubt, Smoky thought looking at it, what the woman had died of. And there was a good possibility that this had something to do with last night's death.

"But I don't understand why," Tommy said in bewilderment. "You can get legal abortions, for God's sake. Why would anybody do it this way?"

"Because she couldn't afford it. Or because she was being blackmailed and was scared. Or because—there are reasons, Tommy. She might not even know they are legal now. We still don't know who she was."

He opened the top drawer in a dresser, and there was an envelope, a light bill, addressed to Mary Jean Thomas. "So we assume she was Mary Thomas," he said, and blinked his hot, dry eyes. He knew Mary Thomas. She'd been a whore a long time, but she'd never left Farmer's Mound even for the bright lights you could see on the horizon when the night was clear. Mary had been—cute —ten years ago, when he first saw her. People said she'd been pretty, fifteen years ago. He'd tried to talk sense into her; he'd even found her a decent job a couple of times. But she thought she'd found the easy way, until it was too late for her to change. Then she'd gone to hitting the bottle bad, and after a while nobody wanted Mary, even for five dollars, unless he was so down on his luck he couldn't get anything better.

Well, apparently somebody had still wanted Mary. Unless, of course, Mary was the abortionist, and that, considering Eddie's story, didn't seem likely.

He didn't relish having to tell Audra about this, because the hell of it, the part he tried not even to let himself remember, was that Mary was Audra's sister. Audra had loved her, had cared about her. But when the two were left destitute just out of high school by the death of their shiftless father, Audra had gone to work as a waitress, and Mary had tried to find an easier job. Although she had been out of their lives for years, he knew that Audra would take this hard.

He guessed he'd rather tell Audra than wait and let her read it in the newspaper. "Tommy," he said, "you want me to go with you to look for Eddie, or do you think you could find him better on your own?"

"If you've got something else you need to do," Tommy said, "I can find him if he's still in town. But I think I better take a walkie-talkie with me."

"I think so too," Smoky said. "This is one thing you haven't had a chance to learn yet, and you need to. Don't ever feel funny about calling for a back-up unit. Sure, somebody might laugh at you, but whoever it is, he'll be calling for a back-up himself one day too. If there is any doubt whatsoever about the safety of a situation, get somebody to go with you. Come on, let's go back into the station."

On arrival, he marched Tommy back into the dispatch room. "Erik," he said, "this is Tommy. He belongs to us. He's been working undercover, but he got burned last night."

"Hi, Tommy," Erik said. "Looks like they smeared you all over the landscape."

"Part of it, anyway," Tommy agreed.

"He's got work to do," Smoky said, "and he'll be answering to Baker five." Because Smoky at the moment, for reasons best known to others than himself, was answering to car five. "Now I have some personal business to take care of," he told Tommy, and handed him the keys to the brown Fury. "So I'll use my personal vehicle." But, Tommy noticed, he took a radio with him.

Sliding under the wheel of the unmarked car, Tommy suddenly caught sight of his watch and realized the date for the first time. It was his twenty-third birthday. He guessed there was probably a card from his mother in the mail he hadn't looked at for four days. He'd never told Melissa when his birthday was, and there was nobody else to care.

He could barely remember his twenty-second birthday, and he couldn't remember his twenty-first at all. He'd misplaced it somewhere, in the fog all his days became four years ago. But he guessed he'd never forget this, his first day spent working openly as a cop.

He stopped in front of a big, dilapidated grey frame house. Jo Ann Reno came to the door, in an old house-dress and gold-mesh house shoes, with her long greying brown hair straight and stringy around her shoulders. Looking at her, Tommy felt a twinge of pity. She couldn't have been more than fifteen when her first son was born, a long time ago, when Joe and Jo Ann Reno were a cute couple; now, at forty-four, she was a worn-out old woman. Tommy produced the badge. "I need to talk to Eddie," he said.

"Eddie ain't here."

"Do you know where he is?"

"He's left. He come home last night about twelve-thirty and said he'd just found out you was a cop and he had to get out of town. So he packed up a few of his clothes and he left by one-thirty."

And his bike wasn't in the yard. Tommy had no reason

to doubt her. Last night his own gun had been in Eddie's hand and hate and fear had been in Eddie's eyes. He might have known Eddie would run.

"Thanks," he said, and went back down the stairs, wondering who else might have some idea where the car containing the body was. Remembering how secretive Eddie had been, he didn't guess anybody else but the killer knew. Feeling very self-conscious, because he'd never used the police radio before in his life, he took it out of the pouch on his belt and held it up before his face. "Headquarters, this is Baker five."

"Go ahead, Baker five." The dispatcher's voice was quite matter-of-fact.

"Put me a lookout on Eddie Reno. I guess records will have his description."

"Ten-four, Baker five. What is the lookout for?"

He knew Smoky had taken a warrant weeks ago on Eddie, holding it to be served when all the arrests were being made at once. "Violation of the state drug laws."

"Ten-four, do you want that just local, or put on TCIC?"

"Put it on TCIC and NCIC. We'll extradite if need be." That, he was well aware, wasn't usual for a drug case. But right now that heroin he had bought from Eddie weeks ago was the least important thing on his agenda. He wanted, badly, to talk to Eddie about the blood in the little house on Fourth Street.

Jo Ann had walked down the stairs behind him. "Tommy, would you tell me how you got to be a cop?" she said with frank curiosity. "I been knowing you for years. And I sure wouldn't have picked you to be no cop."

"Just lucky, I guess," he said noncommittally. Actually that was perfectly true. It had been luck, his coming out the door at that one moment in time when Smoky needed help, and he didn't follow the memory to its logical conclusion—that for him to be a cop now, he had been man enough to give Smoky the help he needed at a time when it was hell for him to try to work. He only thought, gratefully, that nobody could ever have gone farther down that dead-end road and still have been snatched back and put into a responsible life.

It had been so easy, so—it was hard to explain, even to himself. People like the Renos (and he had almost gotten to be like the Renos) took life as it came, they acted almost on instinct, and it had been easy to live like that; a person who'd lived straight all his life could never understand how relaxed that hand-to-mouth, take it where you can get it, life was.

Being a cop would never be easy. A cop has to think. He has to figure things out for himself and make decisions fast and act on them and be prepared to back them up later, not with a gun, not with flying fists, but with words, in a courtroom, knowing a judge who'd never heard a shot or felt a blow might call him wrong for that instant decision that had to be made.

Well. Damn. Eddie had said the corpse was in a car "out the other side of town." Tommy guessed he'd go look out the other side of town.

Captain Cardew listened, without interruption, to Smoky. Then he said, "You're telling me you sent Inman out by himself to look for Eddie Reno? After last night?"

Linn Conner, sitting beside Chuck, blinked. She'd thought it was only the policewomen that people worried about going off by themselves.

"He'll be okay," Smoky said. "He knows how to think."

"Well, this other is peculiar," Cardew said slowly. "I could understand a whore needing a lock picker. But hiding the body like that, and then trying to get a dumbass like Eddie Reno to cover his tracks—I think we'd better give that house the full treatment."

Jerry Duncan, also in the group gathered by Cardew's desk, nodded. The full treatment of a crime scene involved quite a lot of work. It was eleven o'clock now, and with one assistant (he didn't like to confuse the scene by having several people with him), he'd be lucky to get through by nightfall. He looked around the group. "Chuck," he began.

"Oh, shit," Chuck said, "I was afraid you were going to ask me."

"I could go," Linn said. "Chuck's taught me how to use the camera." Linn had been, on paper, a policewoman for two years. But she'd really been serving as a secretary until three months ago, and they hadn't sent her out yet on anything big.

"It smells God-awful," Smoky told her.

"So do baby diapers," Linn said.

"How do you know that?" Chuck inquired, in tones of greatly exaggerated interest. Linn was aggressively unmarried.

"I have a sister, dummy," she replied, "and my sister has a baby, and his pants are just terrible when he wakes up."

"No reason why you shouldn't come along," Jerry said thoughtfully. "But I warn you, if you decide to faint, I'm going to walk over you and keep on going." Which he very probably would do. Jerry Duncan, a Hard-shell Baptist, was also what is known as a hardnosed cop. He had infinite patience with anyone who was trying to learn, but he had no patience at all for what a cop with a less-guarded tongue would call a screw-up.

"Then I'll hit the darkroom," Chuck said, "and get those pictures from last night done." The pictures were of the pathetic little body of Rosemary, huddled bleeding by the pyracantha bush in her front yard where she'd been found five hours after the neighborhood was organized to search for her (which indicated she had been put there while the search was in progress). There were also a few pictures of Tommy Inman, looking like he would never look again, his long brown curls matted with blood.

"I want to go home and get a sandwich," Smoky said, "and Tommy's got my car. I'll be in my own personal vehicle, but I'll have a radio with me."

"I'll be in the darkroom, if anybody needs me," Chuck said.

It won't be easy, Smoky thought again on the way to the car, telling Audra.

Linn's face was a little pale, but she was clearly determined to do exactly as she was told. She noted, very properly in her notebook, the day of the week, time of day, and weather conditions, and then took all the photographs Jerry told her to take (because Jerry and the camera were sworn enemies, and never mind that an old Speed Graphic is a heavy camera to be hand-held by a small woman. Linn wasn't the only woman to use one).

The process of working a crime scene is a long and tedious one. It involves a lot of packaging and labelling things and writing down where they came from; it involves scraping very unpleasant things off walls and floors; it involves fingerprint cameras and fingerprint powder and special vacuum cleaners with filters in them to collect the dust off the floor. It involves careful searches for hairs and fibers and leaves, and anything that does not belong where it is. And all of this is done in inadequate lighting, often in the midst of very bad smells, and it doesn't matter if the evidence technicians are tired or hungry or (as does not happen to Jerry Duncan but often does to other evidence technicians) hung over. The work is precise and exact. It makes no front pages, no TV shows, no murder novels, and usually not over a paragraph in *True Detective* magazine. But it is necessary work.

It would be a long afternoon, in the now much-too-warm and unfragrant house on Fourth Street.

*   *   *

It was the fifteenth field Tommy had stopped at. It still wasn't quite out of the city limits, but it was far in the direction Eddie apparently had been talking about. There was no fence around the field, but a good-size gully marked one edge of it; he'd caught just a glint of metal out of the corner of his eye from somewhere in the bottom of the gully.

Cautiously he tried to scramble down the rough limestone side of the ditch, but he tangled with a tree root and slid a few feet, landing on his behind halfway down, slamming hard against some brushwood that had washed into the gully in the last rain. "Damn!" he gasped, blinking back tears the sharp pain brought to his eyes. The brushwood had caught him in just about the same place as the toe of someone's boot had hit last night. He sat still on the damp stone until he could breathe easily again, and then he got up and even more carefully continued on down to the bottom of the gully.

He walked along it, around the margin of the field, keeping a sharp eye out for snakes. The metal was the flattened wreckage of an old Ford, apparently put there in an effort to slow down erosion. There was no smell, but even so he checked carefully until he was sure the car was empty. Then he walked back to where he had fallen and looked up again. He wasn't one hundred percent sure he could get back up the bank.

Except, of course, that he had to.

Back in the car, he leaned his head on the steering wheel, breathing hard and feeling his heart pounding. Only now was he fully realizing just how bad a beating he'd taken last night; his strength wasn't near up to usual, and that couple of days of sick leave Smoky had offered was beginning to look rather inviting.

But there was one more field he wanted to check before he called it a day. It was way out the Mount Zion Church Road, just inside the city limits. Like the field he'd just fallen in, it was bordered on one side by a steep-banked gully cut into the weathered limestone.

He was sure even before he reached the field that this was going to be it. The buzzards were circling but not landing; there was something dead there that they couldn't get at.

He scrambled down the side of the gully, this time almost oblivious of the pain that was like a hot knife in the side of his chest. "Oh, God!" he said, and backed off, trying hard not to vomit. Then he approached again, forcing himself to look.

It had been a while, and the car was hot and closed so the body fluids hadn't had any way to evaporate. Even with the car closed the stench was unbelievable, and Tommy felt quite sure he was going to be sick when it became necessary to open the car. The body has swollen and burst, and now tattered fragments of flesh and skin clung to the bones. The body was alive with maggots; seething white masses the size of baseballs and larger rolled over and over in frantic ceaseless motion. Tommy stumbled back, away from the car, and reached for his radio. "Baker five to car five." He wondered if his voice sounded as shaky to Smoky as it did to him.

"Go ahead." Smoky's voice, instant sanity.

"Do you know—go to tach two." He had suddenly remembered the existence of tach 2.

"On two," Smoky answered a moment later.

"Do you know where the Mount Zion Church Road is?"

"That's affirmative."

"Come on down it till you see the car parked. I'm down in the gully. I've found—uh—that item."

"Ten-four. Ten-seventy-six."

En route. Tommy sat down in the dirt, far enough back so he couldn't smell it too bad, and waited. Gradually, his breathing and heartbeat settled down to normal, but the pain in his side continued. It felt, with every breath, like somebody was trying to saw one of his ribs out.

Well, Dr. Baldwin had told him last night it wasn't serious, but it would be giving him hell for a week or two. He guessed that was true, if it was going to be like this for long.

Funny thing, he thought, in the movies it never seems to hurt to get shot or stomped. Or else the people in the movies are supposed to be so tough they don't care if it does hurt.

Tommy cared. But, he guessed philosophically, maybe if there wasn't any pain, there wouldn't be any pleasure either. At 2 P.M., sitting in the dirt in a gully on a sunlit afternoon, he looked back on 2 A.M. with much complacency.

Only he wished Melissa hadn't cried afterward. She told him she didn't know why she cried. She told him she did want to, and he didn't make her do anything that she didn't want to do. She didn't *know* why she was crying and don't worry about it. But he was worried, a little, anyway.

With his head against the limestone bank behind him, he stretched out his legs and, as he had long-ago taught himself to do, he relaxed and almost instantly was asleep.

"Tommy? You okay?"

He opened his eyes. "Yeah, just catching me a little shut-eye." Somewhat stiffly, he got to his feet. "It's this way."

Surveying the car and its contents, Smoky's face was quite impassive, and Tommy, feeling his own insides churning, had no idea his face said no more than Smoky's did, or that Smoky was hating the sight and smell just as much as he was. "Well," Smoky said finally, "it's been about two weeks, I guess. We might better call for somebody from the crime lab on this one. I'm not sure Jerry's got the equipment to deal with it."

The car, like the Ford in the other field, had apparently been put in the gully deliberately, in an effort to slow erosion, quite a long time ago. The license plate on it was orange and black, although the colors had been changed to black and white before Tommy had started school. But somebody who knew the car was there had come, probably about two weeks ago, to stuff the body of the woman inside it. And Smoky, who had known Mary Thomas ten years, could not look at this body and say it was Mary Thomas. It might have been the same size as Mary Thomas. It was probably white. It was probably brown-haired. The eyes—well, some rodent, probably a possum, had gotten into the car at some time, possibly by burrowing through a rusted-out place in the floorboard. Certainly at one time there had been eyes. But now there weren't.

She had no clothes on, so far as Smoky and Tommy could tell. There had been a sheet wrapped around her but the possum (or whatever it was) had gnawed on it and dragged most of it off.

There would be no use trying for fingerprints in the car, and quite likely positive identification on the corpse would have to be made through dental charts. It was, all in all, quite a mess indeed.

And nobody but Eddie Reno knew who had put her here.

"Did you find Eddie?" Smoky asked, still looking at the body.

Tommy told him why he hadn't found Eddie.

Smoky's arm came up, slowly, and for a moment his hand rested on Tommy's back. "You should have told me that last night."

Tommy half-shrugged. "Didn't see that it was necessary. Don't let him know I told you. I promised not to, and I wouldn't have, if it hadn't been for this."

"What's between you and Eddie I'll leave alone," Smoky told him. "Look, one or the other of us has got to stand by this until some help gets here. Can you, or would you rather I did it?''

"I will," Tommy said, "but would you bring me something to drink?''

"Got a can of Coke in the car, if you want to walk up there with me," Smoky said. "I thought you might be needing a little restorative, if it was as bad as I figured it'd be.''

"Was it?''

"Yep.''

They got the body out of the car. They got it formally identified as Mary Jean Thomas by the rather grisly expedient of removing the hands and carrying them to Austin, along with her fingerprint card, for the big state lab to deal with. Dr. Hamnet was able to say she had indeed died of what they guessed she died of, and it was possible, though he couldn't say for sure, that the same person killed both her and Rosemary.

There was, he added cautiously, some slight evidence of training. Whoever did it knew what he was doing.

But Eddie stayed missing, and the town was a frustrating maze of nobody-knows-nothing. The farmer who owned the field was out of town for a month, and nobody could be located who would admit to having heard or seen anything either in the field or in the little house on Fourth Street.

The warrants from Tommy's undercover work were served, most of them; a few of his pushers went missing, which he guessed was okay, too, as long as they stayed out of Farmer's Mound. Most of them pled guilty and were put on probation, and, Tommy figured, went right back to selling, only being a little more careful who they sold to.

April ended and May came in, with Tommy in uniform and mostly driving a patrol car. Smoky was now the father of a girl named Kathy, and the boy, who had lately turned five years old, came back from exile to resume his customary perch, complete with purple plush rabbit, on Smoky's lap.

May was half over, and nobody had gotten any further on the murders, and nobody had heard anymore about the almost-forgotten blackmailer dogging David Barnett.

May was being a quiet month.

III

TOMMY SQUARED HIS shoulders. It hurt—how it hurt—but it couldn't wait. He walked into the detective bureau, holding the dark-blue billed hat in his hand. In the blue uniform, with his hair short and his moustache gone, he somehow looked much younger than he had six months earlier. "Captain Simons," he said, "I've got to talk to you in private."

The red-haired captain swiveled his chair around. "Can't it wait till later?"

Tommy swallowed, looked at the two Rangers sitting with the captain, thought of Melissa sitting by the phone, and swallowed again. "No, sir," he said, "it can't wait."

"Excuse me, gentlemen," Simons said. "It appears that this matter takes precedence." He followed Tommy into an interrogation room and slammed the door. "What is it?" he asked tartly. The business he was on was urgent.

Tommy took a deep breath. "Melissa and I are going to get married."

"I sort of thought you were eventually," the captain said, "but—" He stopped, his breathing suddenly ragged. Then he said, softly, "No. I guess I see why it couldn't wait."

Tommy looked down at the hat in his hands, then back up again, breathing through his mouth. The silence was getting much too long. "I—I just don't know what to say to you," he said, the words coming out all in a rush. "I *can't* say I'm sorry about—about the baby—because, don't you see, I can't *be* sorry, because, because, the baby is going to *be* and I can't go around thinking, 'Hey, kid,

I'm sorry you were born.' I just, just, I'm sorry it's like this, that's all.''

Captain Simons forced himself to breathe steadily, tried to slow the furious pounding of his heart. "All right, Tommy, I won't make it worse. Is that what you wanted me to say?''

"I don't know what I wanted you to say," Tommy said, still looking at his hat, focussing on his badge without really seeing it. "It's just—for Melissa—don't make it worse for Melissa, I was a damn fool and I don't care if you kick me from here to the street, but—"

"I don't, by any chance, suppose you raped her?" the captain asked carefully.

Tommy looked up, the blue eyes suddenly wide with shock. "My God, sir, what do you—"

"Then don't try to take all the blame yourself," Captain Simons said curtly. "You're being melodramatic. It wouldn't do any good for me to—what did you say? Kick you from here to the street? It's done. That's all."

"Yes, sir."

Simons ran one hand through his hair. "It's not what I wanted for her. I don't think it's what she wanted. I don't think it's what you wanted. But at this point, it seems to be the way it is. All right. How far along is she? Can you make a pretty good guess?"

"Six and a half weeks," Tommy said instantly. "I know exactly. It was the night Rosemary died. You remember, you stayed up here all that night, trying to find out about Rosemary. I couldn't leave Melissa alone."

"I see," Simons told him softly, thinking about that night, thinking, *and maybe you didn't so much want to be alone either.* "Sit down," he added, "you don't have to keep standing there."

Tommy sat, put the hat on the desk in the corner, and dropped his head in his hands.

"You're sweating," Simons said. "Pretty hot outside?"

"Yeah," Tommy said, not looking up.

Simons put his hands on Tommy's shoulders. "All right, boy," he said softly. "You're not the first pair it's happened to and you'll not be the last. I'll tell you one thing. If you had left Melissa to tell me, for that I would never have forgiven you. But I know you didn't want to hurt Melissa."

"I love her," Tommy said. "I love her so damn much. She was ready to fight the world for me, even before I could tell her I—I wasn't what I looked like. God knows I want to marry her. I just—I just—it's not right to make her have to marry me. That's what's so rotten about this, that it's taken away her freedom to choose anything except to make the matter worse, and she wouldn't do that. Not Lissa."

"Go to her—you are off duty now, aren't you?"

"Yes," Tommy said, "and I told her I'd be there as soon as I'd talked to you."

Simons took another breath, telling himself to keep the thing in proportion in his mind. "All right," he said, "tell her you talked to me. Tell her I'll be home when I can, but I just can't get away right now. Can I give you some advice now, man to man, and never mind that we're talking about my daughter?"

"I would appreciate any advice. I might—" It was an attempt at humor. "I might not follow it."

"I think you'll follow it. There's no use worrying about it now. The matter's done. It's too late in the afternoon to see about your marriage license; that'll have to wait till your day off. Right now—" His jaw tightened for a moment before he went on. "I'm busy with these Rangers. We've got something working; I'll tell you about it later and I might want your help. I won't be home till about ten o'clock. Why don't you go and remind her how she got that way? I think right now she needs you, not me, just so long as she knows she's still got a dad."

Tommy picked up his hat. "Yes, sir," he said.

Simons swung the door open. "Now git; I've got work

to do." He walked back out to the Rangers. "A minor domestic crisis," he said.

One of the Rangers looked at him sharply; the tone and the expression didn't seem to match, and that patrolman who'd just gone out the door looked mighty upset. But he put it out of his mind. They had work to do. He leaned forward, speaking softly, gesturing with cupped hands. "Now the way I've got it figured is this—"

Simons had dinner at the Sizzler with the Rangers and escorted them to their room at the Holiday Inn. Then he went to the Last Chance Package Store and bought a bottle of Harwood Canadian and a carton of 7-Up. He didn't keep whiskey in the house usually, but there were times, and he figured this was one of them.

He stopped by the front door for a minute and looked at his watch. Ten-fifteen. And the car he drove made enough noise anyway. He opened the door.

They were on the couch in the living room. Tommy had on faded blue jeans and if he was wearing anything else it wasn't visible. His feet were stretched out on the coffee table, and Simons, with a wave of highly unaccustomed pity, could still even six weeks later make out fading yellow bruises on his chest showing every link of the bicycle chain he'd been beaten with. Melissa was curled on the couch with her head in his lap; she was wearing something made of pleated yellow chiffon that Simons had never seen before. "Hi, Daddy," she said drowsily.

"Hi, Lissa," he said. "That's a fetching nighty. Is it new?"

"Yes, Tommy got it for me today."

"Tommy once in a while shows a streak of good sense," Simons remarked lightly, determined to let Melissa set the note for the conversation.

Melissa sat up, the long blond hair falling over her shoulders, and looked up; the expression on her face was one he could remember from when she was four years old

48

and had been caught snitching cookies after promising not to.

Simons sat down on the other side of her. "It's all right, Lissa," he said. "Your mother would know how to say it. I don't. Just, it's all right. Nobody's mad, at you or at Tommy."

She leaned forward, head on her knees, hair falling forward over her face. "I goofed," she said with a catch in her voice.

Tommy put his hand over hers. She squeezed it, then let go.

Simons got up and went to the kitchen, taking his sack with him. He came back a moment later precariously balancing three glasses. Tommy looked at them. "I don't usually drink," he said doubtfully.

"I never," Melissa began.

"It won't hurt you," Simons said. "Either of you. I want both of you to listen to the old man for a minute, okay? You're both feeling like hell, and it looks to me like each of you is trying to take all the blame. Forget about blame. Nobody has to blame anybody. You're young and you love each other and the rest of it, sometimes, follows naturally. What else is wrong? Lissa—in words. How bad is it? Tommy has a right to know."

"I can't be a doctor," she said. "Not now. Not for a long time. Maybe not forever. Because the closest medical school is in Fort Worth and I can't leave Tommy and the baby and go over there, and it's too far to commute. I've been worrying about it for months anyway, because I already knew I couldn't leave Tommy that long and I didn't know what to do about it. I don't have to worry about it anymore. Now I know. So here's what I can do."

She sat up, pushed her hair back. "I can still get to school in Denton through this semester and the summer session. The next semester I won't have any business trying to drive. After that, I want to keep the baby with me all the time for a while. But later, when he—she—the baby is old enough to go to nursery school, I can go back to college. I can still be a nurse. And there's a real interesting new nursing field called nurse practitioner, and they do a lot of the things doctors used to do, and I think I can get into it. Or, they're trying to get a lot more nurse-midwives, there are just a very few now, and I could do that. There's a whole lot of things I can do, without neglecting Tommy or my baby. No, it won't mess up my life. It—I guess it kind of simplifies it. Because I do love Tommy. I do want my baby. And if it's a girl I want to name her Rosemary."

The tears she'd been holding back for nearly seven weeks came then, finally, and Tommy held her. She sobbed for a couple of minutes and then pulled away from him, to drop her head back down on her knees. "Only —only—I never wanted Tommy to have to marry me!"

Simons sat down on the floor in front of her. "Melissa."

"What?"

"Listen to me. No, don't, listen to Tommy instead. Tommy, what were you saying to me this afternoon?"

"I said—" Tommy wasn't touching her. "I said I don't want Melissa to have to marry me. I want her to want to. Melissa, you know as well as I do that's *not* the only answer to this. But I love you, and—and—Lissa, not long ago I saw a baby that nobody wanted a long time before it was supposed to be born, and—and—"

"I would never," Melissa began, and curled up against him, sobbing.

"No. I know you wouldn't. Okay, it's okay, it's all okay now—"

Steve Simons went to his kitchen to make another drink. Then he went up the stairs to his bedroom.

Kathy was asleep, which was unusual. Smoky and Audra were just about to decide Kathy was never, never, never going to learn how to sleep more than five minutes at a time. But she was apparently settled in for a while, and

Lee was also asleep, cuddled on the couch with the purple rabbit.

Smoky was leaning back in the brown recliner chair in his living room, with Audra asleep in his lap. She was so damn thin now, he thought. Of course she'd always been thin; he remembered the first time he saw her she'd looked like a skinny little girl playing dress-up in waitress clothes, but now he doubted she'd weigh over ninety pounds. He offered to get her some household help, but she turned it down, saying that she couldn't sleep with the baby crying anyway, and she guessed the baby would start sleeping through the night eventually.

Well, the baby had been sleeping about an hour now, and Audra had been sleeping most of the hour, too.

The phone rang. Smoky jumped, Audra jumped, and Kathy started howling. "Damn," Smoky said, and vowed to get a bell-chime put in tomorrow.

"Damn," Audra said, which was unusual, as she didn't often cuss. She went toward the bedroom. The phone kept ringing, and Kathy kept howling.

Smoky picked up the phone. "Hello?"

"Smoky?"

"Yeah?" The voice sounded vaguely familiar, but he couldn't quite place it.

"Dave Barnett. Remember me?"

"Yeah, I remember you." How in the hell could anybody forget Dave Barnett? Smoky would be glad when that election was over, though he had to admit Smithers was doing most of the screaming.

"I need to talk to you. And I'm sorry, but it can't wait till morning."

"Can you make it over the phone, or do you need to see me?"

"Over the phone, right now, if you don't mind."

He still wasn't one hundred percent sure he recognized that voice. He damn sure didn't want to be talking with a representative of Smithers thinking he was talking with

Barnett. But there was something he'd wondered about, and the answer would probably tell him for sure who he was talking with. "Look," he said, "can I ask you a dumb question?"

"Ask."

"I've talked with you a time or two, but not enough for me to place your voice all that well. Would you tell me something? How come you don't—I mean, I wouldn't expect you to sound like a field hand, I don't mean that, but you don't sound black at all."

There was what sounded like wry laughter at the other end of the line. "I can still speak black English, Smoky, which you have the intelligence to know exists. But I am an attorney, remember? Juries tend not to believe a person who sounds as if he lives in a ghetto. And as a politician, I am more likely to impress voters if I sound reasonably well educated. And—you're unusual. Most people don't recognize the existence of black English. Yes, I can still use it when I need it."

"I understand," Smoky said. "All right, what's the problem?"

"It's the—the nut," Barnett said. "I—let me start from the beginning. Do you remember when the Autumn Hill Neighborhood Rehabilitation Program was first proposed? I opposed it, rather vehemently, and then changed my mind. The reason was entirely personal. I had a—a rather bad thing happen in Autumn Hill when I was a youngster. I was delivering groceries, and—"

In carefully chosen words, he built a picture for Smoky, the woman bleeding on the floor, the man turning, falling. He finished, "And I guess it was just fear, fear that the knife, with my name on it, would be found. It has been found. A couple of construction workers found it and saw an opportunity for publicity, so they took it to the newspaper. Matt saw it as a human interest story. I saw no way of refusing him without giving a reason, so I let him take his pictures."

"Let me get this straight," Smoky said. "Are you trying to tell me this knife with your name on it has been lying in the bottom of a construction pit since 1941 and isn't rusted away?"

"Apparently it got out of the pit. The metal is rusted some. But it was a hunting knife, and the bone handle, which is very much intact, had not only my name but also my birthdate on it."

"I see," Smoky answered. "Where is the knife now?"

"Matt kept it." He took a deep breath. "I guess it's illogical to wonder, after so many years, but what's the police department position on this?"

"I'm no lawyer."

"I am an attorney. What I asked was the police department view. I can't begin to figure out my legal position, until I find out the course of the investigation."

"I'll have to look up the case," Smoky said, "and frankly I'm not sure the files from 1941 are still in existence, though technically there's no statute of limitations on murder. But if it happened the way you say it did, you certainly have nothing to worry about."

"That is exactly the way it happened," Barnett said. "But I've been thinking about it. Smoky, I'm not really sure he died. He—I—it's like I was in shock. When I went back, to get the knife and wash my hands, the more I think about it, the more I can't remember his being there. Would it be possible?"

"Barely," Smoky said, "but people survive very astonishing things sometimes. Let me get this straight. Are you saying you think maybe he did survive and maybe he's the person hassling you? That sounds very damned farfetched, if you don't mind my saying so. And I can't see how anybody but him could possibly connect that knife to that incident."

"Would you please, in the morning, look up that case file for me and check?"

"I don't quite know what you want me to check on,"

Smoky said, "but I'll look for it. What was her name?"

"Libby, I'm sorry, Libby is all I know."

"Can you give me a date it happened?"

"That I can do. It was July eighteenth."

"Was she black or white?"

"White. And the guy who killed her, he was white too."

"Okay," Smoky said, "I'll see what I can find out about it. But don't you worry about it, for crying out loud."

"I'll—okay. I'll try not to worry about it."

Smoky hung up the phone and considered taking it off the hook. But that didn't seem like a very good idea, because when he did that they usually sent a uniform man to knock on his door. That was even more annoying than a phone call.

Well, at least Kathy had decided to go back to sleep. Audra had gone on to bed while he was on the phone. He guessed he'd take a shower and join her.

If the sound of the shower didn't wake up Kathy. That had to be the yellingest baby in Texas.

Steve Simons came down the stairs at 6:30 A.M., in a brown suit and a very worn brown holster. He stopped short, blinking. "I usually eat breakfast at the coffee shop," he stated.

"I know you do," said Tommy Inman. "That's why I had to go to the grocery store at five-thirty this morning."

Simons sat down at the table. "Well, make yourself at home," he said. After a moment he added, "Seriously. This is a damn big old house for me to rattle around in by myself. You kids might as well stay here. If you won't feel like I'm an albatross." Melissa looked at Tommy, and Simons added, "My bedroom's at the other end of the hall from yours. And I won't feel like taking sides when you two want to have a fight. I get dragged into too many other people's fights as it is."

54

Tommy said slowly, "You're no albatross. I don't see why not. For a while anyway."

Melissa got up and went in the kitchen, shouting over her shoulder, "Y'all eat! I have to leave for school in exactly fifteen minutes and I want the dishes in the sink first."

"You come eat too," Tommy answered.

"I can't," she said. "Eggs don't smell so good today. Oh! Eggs smell awful!" A door slammed in the back of the house.

"I shouldn't laugh," Tommy said, hand to his forehead. "I know she's miserable, but—" Looking highly amused, he got up to follow her.

Thirty minutes later Melissa, having finally managed toast and a 7-Up, was headed for Denton in the yellow Volkswagen, and the men were back in the house. Tommy unplugged the coffeepot. "What do you want me to call you?" he asked abruptly. "I mean, calling you 'captain' across the breakfast table is a little bit silly."

"My name is Steve. And when you get through unloading and reloading, move it, we're late to muster. Do you do that every morning?"

"Yeah," Tommy said. "I heard about a guy that didn't look after his gun, and one day he went to fire it and he couldn't because the bullets had corroded in the cylinder."

"Yipe. Come along and ride with me today."

IV

THE WORK OF a police department in even the smallest town goes on unabated, hour after hour, day after day, year after year. The policeman in next year's black and white sedan, wearing a wash-and-wear synthetic uniform shirt, carrying a stainless steel .38, is the lineal (and sometimes direct) descendent of the last century's town marshal with his sugerloaf hat and heavy .45. The crimes change only slightly: husbands and wives still fight each other, drunks still shoot up bars, and if yesterday's horse thief is today's auto thief the intent is still the same.

Answering calls is dependent not on the weather, the day of the week, the time of day, or the mood of the police. When something new goes down, it does not matter how much more is already going on; the call must be answered, and answered immediately. Perhaps the laws create the crime; perhaps society creates the background; but in the end, it is the criminal who creates the situation. Ideally, it is ultimately the cop who controls the situation. But life doesn't always work out as planned.

Tommy Inman and Charles Harrison were north car. They were ten-seven at Loretta's Truck Stop in the middle of the morning. Tommy had a cup of coffee and Charles, who long-ago had explained that his church didn't approve of coffee or tea, was drinking lemonade, when the radio said, "Ten-three, ten-thirty-three. North car, report of a signal eight in progress at the Jiffi-Mart on Sixth. East car, back them up."

"Ten-four." Because you don't say "I'm ten-seven," and you don't say, "I don't want to go." Ten-three, ten-thirty-three means major emergency, halt normal radio transmission. They dropped quarters onto the table and ran, and if their tires didn't squeal out of the parking lot it was because Charles Harrison was a very good driver.

It had taken Smoky two hours to find out where the 1941 files had been put, and he was sneezing in the dust of decades when the call came. "Hell," he said, and bolted down the hall, fishing his car keys out of his pocket as he ran. A robbery in progress call needs all the help it can get.

Steve Simons was closeted with the Rangers again. The case they were on looked like it was snowballing into something bigger than they'd thought to start with, which had been plenty. He didn't have a radio with him. He figured the dispatcher could use the land line if he was needed anywhere. Only the dispatcher had forgotten where he was.

Chuck and Linn were off, because it was Thursday, and Thursday is usually the quietest day of the week. That left Jerry Duncan to answer calls. He guessed he'd better go to the Jiffi-Mart. Jerry Duncan particularly did not like answering robbery-in-progress calls. Seven months is not long enough for a man to forget the feel of a .45 bullet, and that was how long it had been since he met one, when he accidentally walked in on a robbery in progress.

North car swung down Sixth, and the dispatcher said, "All units, be on the lookout, signal eight suspect vehicle is a red 1976 Mustang, license plate unknown. Four black males occupying vehicle. Use extreme ten-zero as subjects are heavily armed, at least one sawed-off shotgun. Stand by for further."

"There he goes," Tommy said, and Charles swung the black and white in a wide tire-squealing arc, hitting the switch to cut on his lights and siren as Tommy said into the radio, "North car is in pursuit, subject vehicle is headed—Jesus!" A jagged hole had suddenly appeared in

57

the windshield, and glass fragments were everywhere.

Tommy reached around to get the shotgun off the rack behind the seat.

"Ten-nine your location, north car?"

Both Tommy's hands were busy with the shotgun. Charles, steering with his left hand and feeling the car fishtail in the road, fumbled with his right hand for the radio Tommy had dropped on the seat.

"North car, what is your location?" the dispatcher said again, his voice sounding urgent.

"Shut up and I'll give it to you," Charles snarled, and then keyed his mike and gave his location, adding, "This vehicle is being fired on. Stand by."

"All cars, north car is under fire, officers need help—"

Every police car in Farmer's Mound would be coming to them. But the catch on the shotgun rack was jammed and Tommy couldn't get it loose; meanwhile, somebody in the Mustang had the same idea, and Charles could see the muzzle of that shotgun coming out the window. The broad expanse of Tommy's back, with him half kneeling and struggling with the shotgun rack, would make a perfect target—"Get down, Tommy," he said, and passed his own pistol from his right hand to his left, now trying to shoot and drive at the same time.

Tommy whirled around and fired his .38 out the window and ducked down behind the dash. And then it felt like the engine exploded, and the car spun sideways and kept on spinning, and both men leaped out with the car still spinning to look back at a flaming police cruiser.

"Oh my God," Tommy said. "I don't even know what happened."

"The shotgun. He put a solid slug in our engine block and then I think he put another one in our gas tank. Are you okay?"

"Yeah, are you?" Tommy asked, discovering two badly scraped knees and a cut shoulder.

"Yeah," said Charles, who was in a similar condition.

But the Mustang was gone. Charles raised the radio he'd somehow managed to hold onto, and said, "Get us a fire truck over here. Our car's on fire. Slow down the other units. Tell them to look for the Mustang. We lost it."

"I know what happens when you wreck police cars," Tommy said, "but what do you suppose happens when you get one shot out from under you?"

"I don't know," Charles said. "I never did it before." After a moment he added, "I never heard of anybody else doing it, either." He sat down on the curb and dusted his pants, where he'd rolled on the street getting clear of the car.

Tommy sat down beside him. He didn't try to dust his pants, and he wondered why Charles bothered.

It was a quiet residential street, with neatly painted houses and bright blooms of roses and marigolds. People were beginning to gather, to look at the blazing wreck and at the two policemen sitting on the curb. Nobody seemed to know what to say to them. So nobody said anything.

Sergeant Lew Jarvis drove up beside them and got out. "What in the hell happened to you two?" he asked.

They told him.

"You didn't by any chance get the license plate of the Mustang?"

"I wrote it down on my clipboard," Charles told him gloomily. "Which is on the seat. Or was."

Jarvis turned to look at the cruiser. He shook his head.

A brown Fury parked behind the uniform car, and Smoky O'Donnell got out. He looked at the fire, and he looked at the two patrolmen. "You get in more damn trouble," he told Tommy, as a fire truck screamed up the street.

"Yeah," Tommy said. And then he said, "I just remembered the license number. It's—"

Radio informed them it had been reported stolen two hours ago. And for the moment it had gotten clean away with $120 from the Jiffi-Mart, leaving behind one flaming patrol car and two badly shaken patrolmen.

A CB'er spotted the Mustang, thirty-five minutes later, parked on Denton Road, and Jerry went out to check it for fingerprints. He'd already dusted what few things they'd handled in the Jiffi-Mart and found only glove marks. He figured that was all he'd find in the Mustang.

The CB'er hadn't stopped, he'd just noticed the license plate and kept going, radioing the location of the vehicle over the CB Emergency Channel 9 to Farmer's Mound React, and nobody had looked inside the Mustang until Jerry got there.

Jerry was quite astonished by what he found in the car. What he found was Harry Evans, a well-known local burglar. And Harry Evans was dead. Judging from the apparent trajectory of the bullet, and the location of the blood and brain tissue in the car, it was probably Tommy who killed him.

If it was Tommy it was going to be rough on him. That, Jerry remembered, was the thing Tommy had worried the most about when he was deciding whether he wanted to be a cop.

The telephone rang in the detective bureau and kept on ringing. Steve Simons, who did not want to be disturbed by the telephone, glared at it and answered it.

"Is Smoky O'Donnell there?"

"Let me check," he said, and flung open the door, ready to yell at anybody he saw.

He didn't see anybody.

"No," he said into the phone, "he's not. Can I help you?"

"No, I'd rather talk to Smoky. He's familiar with the situation. Do you know when he might be there?"

"No, sir, I don't. Could I have him call you back?"

"No, that's all right. I'll get in touch with him later. Thank you."

That call disposed of, Simons called the dispatcher.

"Where in hell are all my detectives?"

"Well, I guess they're all out on that shooting."

"That—what shooting?"

"Well, that holdup man."

"What holdup man? What the hell is going on?"

The dispatcher told him what was going on. Simons couldn't think of anything profane enough to say, so he didn't say anything. "I've got to go out awhile," he told the Rangers. And he went. Without inviting them, which was silly of him, as they of course got in their car and followed him.

Cops tend to be nosy.

All cops.

They'd got the fire out, finally, but the car was still too hot to move. Simons looked at it, and he thought of Tommy Inman sitting on the couch last night in faded blue jeans, and quite suddenly he knew why some police departments won't hire two members of the same family. It was very hard to feel objective about this.

He drove on out Denton Road.

There were altogether too many police gathered around the Mustang. As senior man present, he chased half of them off, and then looked inside at the body. "I'm glad it was him and not one of you," he said. "I swear I don't know how either one of you got out of that car in one piece."

Jerry Duncan was writing in a notebook. Then he put it in his pocket, to begin taking pictures so that the EMS crew could move the body.

Smoky walked over to Simons. "I need to get back in," he said. "You want me to transport these two yardbirds in and sit them down to write out statements?"

"Yeah, might as well. What have you got that's so urgent?"

"Tell you later. Come on, you two squirrels."

He ambled back to car five, followed by two patrolmen. Harrison, who knew Smoky O'Donnell only by sight, was trying to figure out whether or not he approved of a lieutenant who called him "squirrel" and "yardbird." Tommy figured if he was being called that sort of thing he wasn't in trouble. He'd already had a few servings of the kind of names Smoky called people he was really mad at.

A mile down the road he said, "Smoky, I'm gonna be sick!"

Smoky pulled onto the dirt shoulder and stopped the car. Tommy scrambled out and quite thoroughly was sick. When he was through, he leaned on the fender, panting, and wiped his face with a handkerchief. When he was breathing evenly again, he got back in the car, dropping his head on his knees. "Worry," he said, "I think I got me a kind of reversible stomach."

"At least you warned me. You shouldn't have looked that close at him."

"Well, I had to," Tommy said. "And I didn't get sick at that one in the car in the gully."

"No, but you didn't kill that one, either," Smoky told him. "You can vomit up your toenails, Tommy, but you can't get rid of it, so you might as well accept it."

"Did you ever kill anybody?"

"No," Smoky said.

"I did," Charles said surprisingly. "When I was a law enforcement Explorer Scout, of all crazy things. Somebody opened fire on the man I was riding with. He landed on the ground and I grabbed the shotgun. I was seventeen then, and I think I spent a week crying to my bishop before he could convince me I wasn't going straight to hell for it. You won't forget this one. But you'll get over it."

"I sure hope so," Tommy said dubiously.

"You have to, Tommy," Smoky said patiently. "And you know it. This one, I've been knowing him as long as I've been policing in this town. And he's no loss."

"No. I know. It's just reaction."

"As long as you realize that," Charles told him. "Because there's no place in the Bible that really, if properly translated, says, 'Thou shalt not kill.' What it says is, 'Thou shalt not murder.' And there's a difference.''

"I guess," Tommy said. He'd never thought about that part of it at all. He just knew he didn't want to kill anybody.

The car stopped in the little dirt parking area that was reserved for the detective cars. Out of the car, Tommy grinned, suddenly, at Smoky. "Man, if I'd known what I was getting into when I came out the door that day—!"

"Would you have still done it?"

"Hell, yes!"

Smoky left them writing reports and went back to the dusty hot little room where the old files were. And to his own surprise, he found the one he was hunting.

What he read caused him to sit back on his heels, frowning in puzzlement. Then he picked up the whole file and headed for the detective bureau; Tommy met him in the hall, to inform him that David Barnett was on the phone for him.

"Good," Smoky said, "because I need to talk to him, too." He walked on into the detective bureau and picked up the phone. "O'Donnell here."

"Can you come out to my house right away? It's urgent that I show you—"

"On the way," Smoky said, "because I've got some things to show you, too."

The man who killed women sat in his living room, turning pictures over in his mind. Libby Bonner had been the first in Farmer's Mound, and she had come close to being the last anywhere, but there had been no strength in the boy's arm, and the cut, though painful and bloody, had not been deep. He'd known then who the boy was, but he'd had to get out of town until the wound healed, because he figured the police might notice someone with a bad cut.

But before he left, he'd set the stage for accusing the boy. He already knew he liked killing, but he hadn't meant to kill that one—hadn't meant to because he could be connected with her—but it had just happened, he did kill her, and nobody made the connection. He would get the boy one day anyhow, he told himself then. But what with one thing and another, it had been many years before he saw Farmer's Mound again.

The war had taken him overseas. He remembered a prostitute in Germany, a barmaid in Austria. After that his job had kept him moving. He'd killed a couple of other women in Autumn Hill on his infrequent trips home, but somehow he never, on those trips, thought of the boy.

He'd learned how to do abortions because they brought him a good supply of women, women who had covered their tracks before coming to him. He liked abortions even when he didn't kill the woman, because there was blood and a form of death and sometimes the women screamed. But every now and then he killed one anyway. Just because he could.

He'd finally come home to Farmer's Mound six months ago. And he needed women for use, not just for killing. He'd used Mary Thomas before, on one of his earlier trips home, so he went to her at first. Then he'd found the girl, the pretty little girl with the teenage body and almost no mind at all to protest, to remember. But he'd miscalculated badly on both of them—and then he killed, and they were the most exciting of all the killings he'd done, because it was like killing part of himself and still being alive.

There was more killing he wanted to do. But in the midst of his arrival home there'd come the shock of learning that nearly forgotten David Barnett, who'd left him scarred like this, was not, as he should be by now, a broken-down field hand or day laborer. He was wealthy, a lawyer, and so respected a politician that even white people liked him.

That disgusted the killer. It was a situation that could not be allowed to continue.

He'd set the stage for it many years ago. Now he was beginning to set the wheels in motion. And if he'd guessed right about how Barnett would react—

It was a Xerox copy of an old newspaper clipping. Printed on the paper above the clipping was "We know what happened, don't we? The police knew you were there. And we know who had a knife." Paperclipped to it was the new clipping, Matt's story about the knife found in Autumn Hill.

"Do you suppose he thinks he'll make me think I did it?" Barnett asked, sounding puzzled.

The old clipping was for July 19, 1941.

GRISLY MURDER IN VICE DISTRICT
POLICE SEEK CLUES IN GHASTLY CRIME

Overlook police today are still searching for some indication of the identity of the person who yesterday committed the atrocious slaying of attractive young Elizabeth Bonner, a resident of the Autumn Hill section of this city.

(Badly overwritten, Smoky thought, as he read on.)

The nude and mutilated body of the brunette divorcee was discovered in her living room about 7:00 P.M. by police responding to an anonymous telephone call. The body appeared to have been subjected to repeated blows from some blunt instrument, as well as being savagely slashed with a knife.

Police surmise a second person also was wounded, as a considerable quantity of blood was found in another part of the room.

Smoky put the paper down.

"I don't understand any of that," Barnett told him. "There weren't any knife wounds on her. And I know she had a dress on. And why does he think the police know I was there? I mean, I told you, but—"

"Listen to this," Smoky said, and read aloud from the yellowed report. " 'Davey Barnett, Negro/Male twelve years old, delivery boy from Shelton's Grocery, interviewed. Stated he left groceries at house about 3:00 P.M., picked up grocery list for next day, did not see victim, states everything looked normal.' Now tell me, did you talk to—"

"A guy asked me some questions," Barnett said, "but he wasn't—" He stopped. "Oh, my God. I'm sorry. I was twelve years old and I was scared. He didn't have a uniform on. And I didn't realize he was a policeman."

"So you lied to him."

"I lied to him. Nobody ever told me who he was. Mr. Shelton just said, 'Hey, kid, come talk to this guy,' and walked off."

"Damn," Smoky said. "Forty-two years. You've put us forty-two years late in hunting this bastard. I hope you realize that. And God knows what all he's done in the meantime. Could you—I realize it's worth damn all now, but could you have picked him out of the mug book then?"

"I could pick him out now," Barnett said, "if I saw a picture of how he looked then. But I don't think that's necessary. Because this was in the mail too. I think he really thinks he could make you think I killed her. Or at least he thinks I'll think he could. Look here."

It was a letter printed crudely by hand. It said, "Put $10,000 in small bills in a locker at the airport. Go to the airport coffee shop and sit in the first booth. When you leave, put the key to the locker on your seat. If you don't I'll be able to make some connections in the cops' minds."

"He reads the el cheapo paperback thrillers," Smoky

said. "Too bad he didn't tell you when he wanted you to do it."

"He telephoned that part of it," Barnett told him. "Tonight at ten o'clock."

"I'll get you a stakeout, if you want to go down there," Smoky told him. "But I don't see any sense you risking the money."

"I figured a briefcase full of newspaper," Barnett said. "I went down to the bank and got a couple of hundred in loose ones to put on top, in case he decides to look inside. I wonder," he added thoughtfully, "if he has any idea how big ten thousand dollars in small bills is."

Involuntarily Smoky chuckled. "I'm sorry," he said, "I know this is damn serious, but of all stupid—"

"Well, it is rather," Barnett said, "but if you'd seen how she looked—"

"Pictures in the file," Smoky told him, and took them out.

Barnett looked, for a moment, and then slowly reached out and picked them up. He looked at them, and Smoky looked at him. He was beginning to frown. "No," he said, "it wasn't—that's not right." He went to the next picture. "That's not right," he said again. "It wasn't like that. Over there on the couch, that's the dress she had on. And she had it *on* when I left. I remember that dress. I was twelve years old, you know, and that's old enough to— you know. I thought Libby was the prettiest thing I'd ever seen, and that dress—it was yellow. And—Oh, my God. My God. It wasn't—she wasn't cut up like that. She wasn't—her head, that's right, it—was like that, her skull was broken like that, there was—Jesus, God, I tried so hard to forget, there was—brains—like that, but she wasn't—my God, did he do that? Or had she been autopsied when this picture—"

"He did that," Smoky said.

"My God," Barnett repeated.

The lower part of the body had been savagely mutilated, and close-up pictures taken in the morgue showed just what the extent of the slashing was. "No autopsy looks like that," Smoky told him. "And I've sure seen my share." He took the pictures back; Barnett's face had gone a blotchy yellow, and it would have been inhuman to ask him to look at anymore.

But after a moment he said, "Look, I've got to ask you this. You could have told us about this any time in the last forty-two years. So why didn't you?"

"It just seemed to get less important, as time went by. I didn't really forget it, but I pushed it farther and farther back in my mind."

"Why didn't you report it to start with?"

"I was panicky, the first day. By the second, there was a letter stuck in my mother's mailbox for me. It didn't go through the mail. It said, 'If you tell I'll make the police think you did it.' Try to understand. I was twelve years old. I was scared. And—it wasn't now."

It wasn't now. Smoky realized what was meant by that. Then, it was quite possible the blame could have been shunted onto a "N/M 12 years old" who just happened to stumble in.

"I see," Smoky told him. "All right. I'll get you a stakeout set up."

The kitchen door opened and a woman entered, carrying a sack of groceries. She paused. "Cynthia, you know Smoky," Barnett told her.

"Sure. Hi. Can I make you some coffee?"

This was Smoky's first close look at Cynthia Barnett, and he liked what he saw. She was very small, very pretty, and probably fifteen years younger than her husband. "No, thanks," he told her, "you're busy, and I need to get on this little matter your husband was telling me about."

"Yes," she said, "I know about that little matter. All right. Another time, then."

*   *   *

In the car on the way home, Simons commented, "It scared the hell out of me when I heard what you'd been in today."

"Did it? I wasn't any too happy about it myself."

"I'm just as glad I didn't know when it was going on," Simons added. "I was so tied up with the Rangers I didn't even hear about it till an hour after it happened. That's why I was so late getting out there. Listen, how would you feel if I asked Melissa to do a spot of, oh, call it undercover work?"

"That's up to Melissa," Tommy said. "I damn sure don't want her hurt. But I know you wouldn't ask her if there was any risk involved."

"I don't feel there is. I'll wait and explain it to you both at once. No sense going through it twice."

They pulled into the driveway beside the yellow Volkswagen that was parked under an oak tree in the front yard. Tommy walked into the house. "Hi, Lissa, we're home."

She turned. "Hi."

"You look tired," Tommy said.

She came to his arms, not saying anything.

"Hey, Lissa, got an arm for the old man?"

She stretched one arm toward him. "Hi, Daddy. I was just worried when I got home and y'all weren't here."

"Ah, people just naturally are late every now and then," Tommy said.

"And this time," Steve said, "we were just late because we had some paperwork to finish up, and then we stopped by the grocery store so this man of yours wouldn't have to haul his can out again in the predawn hours to buy eggs."

"Good thinking," Melissa said.

Tommy guessed he would have to tell her, before the newspaper came, but he'd wait a little while yet. Because it couldn't not scare her.

"Come on in the living room," Steve told her. "Something's come up I need to talk with you about."

"Okay." She sat down on the floor on a cushion.

"To start with," Steve said, "let me give you some background I want to be sure you understand. In an undercover job you don't get what you pay for. Tommy bought drugs; he didn't use them. A big city vice cop goes into a whorehouse, he pays his money but he doesn't follow through. Understand me?"

"Yes, I know all that. Why are you telling it to me?"

"I wanted to be sure you don't misunderstand what else I'm going to say. Melissa, we think we might know who killed Rosemary."

"Who?"

"His name is George Revills. He moved away from Farmer's Mound a long time ago, way before I was policing. He has a little record, at different times, in different places, for both child molestation and abortion. He moved back to Farmer's Mound about eight months ago. We're pretty sure he's the one who got Rosemary pregnant, though I doubt we can prove it. We can prove he was hanging around down there a lot. We've got a couple of local prostitutes to say he performed abortions on them; they'll testify if we promise them immunity. But we feel like we need a little more. The Rangers have been down here a couple of days, and we've been trying to figure out what to do. We talked about borrowing a policewoman from another town, sending her in, and then us going in. There are two objections to that. One, you take off a wedding ring, it leaves a line. The other, he probably could tell she wasn't really pregnant even with a superficial examination, which of course is as far as we'd let it go."

"I see," Melissa said slowly. "Daddy, you wouldn't really let him hurt my baby?"

"You know better than that."

"What would you want me to do?"

"We have a Ranger that would call in and make arrangements, because he's got the information on how to make the contact. You'd go in, let him look at you, pay him. Then we'd go in. You'd have a little transmitter the size of a cigarette package with you, and we'd be both listening and tape-recording everything that was said. Any time we couldn't hear you, or if anything started to go wrong, we'd be right there." He took a deep breath. "Melissa, I'll tell you the truth, I don't like it at all, and if you don't want to do it nobody will be mad at you. But one of the Rangers asked me if I knew of a local girl just starting a pregnancy who might be able to carry this through. And I knew you loved Rosemary. I thought you might be willing."

"Will Tommy be there?"

"You damn well better not think I'd let you go there without me," Tommy said.

She pondered a little bit longer. "When?"

"Tomorrow."

"Okay," Melissa said. "But now I have to go cook supper."

"I'll go help you," Tommy said. "And I think maybe I'd better tell you what happened today. Before you turn on the television. Because you know how TV people build things up."

Simons went upstairs to change clothes. He did not want to hear that discussion. Melissa had been a cop's daughter all her life.

But now she was going to have to learn about being a cop's wife.

V

A COMMUNICATIONS BREAKDOWN is serious.

It is most serious when nobody knows there is one.

Robert Cardew was chief of detectives. He assumed Steve Simons, who ran the day watch in the detective bureau, was keeping track of the day watch. He was, the best he could.

Besides running the day watch, Steve Simons was working on the murder of Rosemary Waters. Because he knew all that was in the case jacket, he assumed he knew all that was known about that case.

But it was to Smoky O'Donnell, working on the murder of Mary Thomas, that the medical examiner had said, "I think the same person did both of these." And Smoky had the habit of playing a lone hand. He had forgotten to tell anyone else what Dr. Hamnet said.

This time, Steve Simons was playing a lone hand too, because he didn't want to spook his suspect. He hadn't told anybody but Captain Cardew and the police chief what the Rangers were doing in Farmer's Mound.

It should've begun to come together, because Tommy Inman had worked closely with Smoky O'Donnell for a year, and tended to keep track of what he was doing. But before dinner-table discussion had a chance to get started, Tommy was called out to the airport for a stakeout. He left the house in blue jeans and a Kermit the Frog sweatshirt, leaving Captain Simons somewhat puzzled as to when and how Tommy's clothes had arrived at his house.

And when Tommy might otherwise have been discussing

murder with his soon-to-be father-in-law, he was in the airport, inquiring vaguely about flights arriving from Atlanta. He explained he didn't know which one his girl was on, or maybe it was Miami or Chicago she was coming in from anyway, so he intended to meet all the planes. He parked himself on a chair, in full view of both the coffee shop and the rental lockers.

The man who liked to kill women was thinking. He couldn't decide about this one. He wasn't sure killing this one would be the best thing to do. He remembered the sound of his cane striking Libby Bonner, when the boy walked in, but he remembered hearing the sound of the knife in his throat. That was what he remembered, the sound, not really the feel at all. . . .

He'd taken the knife the boy left, because it was sharper than his own bone-handled knife, and it was the boy's knife he'd used on Libby Bonner, listening to the sound of the knife slicing her through and through. That was after the boy came and left again, taking the knife the man had dropped when he grabbed the boy's knife.

He'd taken the boy's knife home with him, but then he couldn't remember what he did with it. After that he got the sharp boning knife he'd used on all the others, keeping it honed down to a razor's edge to this very day. He didn't know how many women he'd killed with it, in all these years. He wished he'd kept a diary, besides that partial record of sorts he did keep, but he just hadn't done it, and he couldn't remember them all. He knew it was more than seventy, but he didn't guess it was as many as a hundred and fifty.

He read all the detective magazines, and sometimes he got a kick out of it when they dragged out one of his, wondering again who did it. Sometimes the police in some places made guesses perilously near right, but other times they were so far off it was funny.

But all those women had been loose women. This one wasn't. He just didn't know for sure what he was going to do about this one.

Of course, it was all gambling that the politician would do as he was expected to do. If he didn't, of course, there'd be another way to get at him. But this was such a good plan it would be a shame not to use it, especially after he'd gone to all the trouble. . . .

Tommy had been on a few stakeouts. Most of them he'd spent in very uncomfortable places, such as empty stores, floorboards of parked cars, even a time or two on the ground under a car. This was a more comfortable place, but he was feeling more and more conspicuous. It was just approaching nine o'clock, and nothing could be expected to happen for another hour.

An airport in a town the size of Farmer's Mound is a slow place. People go to it when it is time for their flights to leave, and they leave the airport as soon as their flights land. Very few people were ever in the waiting area. Already a ticket agent or two was beginning to glance his way.

It was a warm late spring night. All over town, things were happening. A pile of big truck tires had been left in the parking lot at Western Auto. Nobody was stealing the tires, but somebody was hiding behind them, putting tape on a pane of glass to muffle the noise. In the morning Western Auto would be missing two television sets.

Two teenage boys were walking through a used-car lot. They hadn't made up their minds, yet, what they wanted to do. They might go to a movie, or they might go play Pac-Man, or they might go joyriding. The decision had already been made for them, by the man who had made sure all the cars were locked up and the keys were put away before he left to go home.

So the boys would go on to a movie, and ten years later

one of them would be a chemist and one of them would be on the Farmer's Mound Police Department, and neither of them would remember the night the decision had been made for them.

In a drugstore, a pharmacist who was up against the wall in both his financial and personal life was locking the narcotics safe. He was alone behind the high counter, and one bottle of cocaine that was supposed to go into the safe went into his pocket instead. It was rather bulky—cocaine is surprisingly lightweight, and an ounce of it fills a good-size bottle. An ounce of cocaine costs about seventy dollars wholesale. He knew where he could sell it for four thousand dollars. He figured the fellow who was buying it from him would turn around, cut it, and sell it for eight thousand dollars. He didn't much care. He planned to be gone.

In another part of town, two boys were walking down an alley. They were walking aimlessly, because they didn't have much to do. One of them spotted a ladder, left where someone had been cleaning out a rain gutter. Above the ladder, the window to the second-floor office of the furniture company had been left half open, out onto the flat roof.

A block away, a black and white was aimlessly cruising, watching the action. Its driver wasn't a blacktop cop, one who sticks to the blacktopped main streets. He knew every alley in town, and just now he was driving with his lights off.

The boys were looking up. "Hey, I wonder what's there," one said, and put his right foot on the ladder.

"Look, man, I don't care what's up there," the other said.

"Well, I just want to go look."

"No way," the other said stubbornly. "Come on, man, we don't need up there."

They walked on down the alley. The driver of the police car had been watching. He had seen the hesitation, deduced the squabble, watched the boys leave. He turned his headlights on and drove slowly on past the ladder, stopping beside them. "Saw you two checking out that ladder," he said. "Some people are mighty careless, aren't they?"

"Um—yeah," one of the boys said.

"Just leavin' that ladder there, with the window wide open! Could have been anybody found it, even a burglar." He pulled out a notebook. "Well, I'm going to call the owner to come down here and lock up. You boys mind giving me your name and address, so's I can let him know who found it for him?"

The field interrogation cards would go to the detectives. For six months, they would be retained. Then they would be thrown away.

Some people make their own futures.

The man who killed women had always made his own future. He had his mind made up, now. He would attack this woman the same way he had attacked Libby Bonner, with a cane. He hadn't used a cane in years. He might just decide not to kill her.

This one time, it might be more fun not to kill.

It was nearly time to leave. He drove to the closest bar, to have him a whiskey before his plan went into action.

The seat at the airport was getting hard, and Tommy didn't like sitting still. He wriggled, miserably, and tried to think about Melissa instead of about how uncomfortable he was.

He didn't like them using Melissa on this thing about the abortionist. Damn, he didn't like it at all; if anything went wrong—

Nothing would go wrong. He wouldn't let himself think that. Nothing could go wrong. Not to hurt Melissa. Not to hurt the baby.

A middle-aged black man came into the terminal. He

was carrying a black briefcase. He walked briskly over to the lockers, dropped two quarters into the slot. He put the briefcase in the locker and shut the door. Then he went on into the coffee shop.

Tommy, keeping the locker in sight, walked over to the Coke machine and fed it a quarter. That might not be a good idea. He was beginning to need to make a pit stop. That is one of the more serious inconveniences of a stakeout. Unless it's a two-man stakeout (and most of them aren't), a pit stop is not usually possible.

On most of them, you also can't get a Coke.

A few minutes later, the black man left. Tommy knew he was now going to the police station, to wait.

Tommy waited. And waited. And waited.

From where he was sitting, he could see the waitress remove the black man's coffee cup and wipe a wet towel over the table, dropping the dollar he'd left under the cup into her apron pocket. She never walked over to the side of the table the man had been sitting on.

At eleven o'clock, the coffee shop closed, and the last person out the door closed and locked it. Tommy could make out the locker key, silver against the blue vinyl of the seat, locked inside.

That posed an interesting problem, he thought.

He kept on waiting.

A few minutes after midnight an airport security guard asked, "Mister, what are you doing?"

"I'm waiting," Tommy said.

"For what?"

"Just waiting."

"Look, mister," the guard told him, "the next plane into here lands at nine A.M. And the next plane out of here leaves at seven A.M. So suppose you find someplace else to wait."

"Oh, shit," Tommy said. He started to reach for identification, and found himself looking into the muzzle of the security guard's .38.

"I saw that gun from across the room," the guard told him. "You keep your hands away from it. Stand up. Real slow."

"I'm a cop," Tommy told him. "I'm a cop. I'm here because I'm trying to keep an eye on a—on a situation."

"And I suppose you can prove that."

"My ID is in my shirt pocket, left side. You reach in and get it." He put his hands on top of his head, interlaced his fingers, and stood quite still.

The guard reached in his pocket, took the passcase out and opened it. He compared the picture on the ID card with the face in front of him. "Yeah," he said.

"Can I put my hands down now?"

"No. Phony ID is too easy come by. Cal!" he said to a second security guard who had walked up to see what was happening. "Call the police and see if they've got a Thomas John Inman and if he's s'posed to be here."

"Talk to Lieutenant O'Donnell," Tommy said. "He's who sent me."

A moment later the second guard, at a telephone booth, called, "He's okay. Hey, Inman, your lieutenant wants to talk to you."

Seeing the first guard holstering his gun, Tommy walked to the phone. After he hung up the guard said, "Hey, look, I'm sorry, but you got to admit, it did look funny."

"It did," Tommy agreed, "and I'd have done the same thing. No hard feelings. They just called me off. My replacement will be out here at five A.M. Don't try to arrest him, okay?"

"My replacement comes on at one o'clock," the guard answered. "I'll give him the message."

"You may as well go home too," Smoky told Barnett.

"Yeah, I guess so," Barnett said. "Well, damn! I sure was hoping this would get him."

78

"Maybe in the morning," Smoky said. "Tommy says the key's still where you left it."

"Is he sure?"

"He says he could see it. We'll have somebody out there in the morning an hour before that coffee shop opens back up."

"Well—okay. If you're sure."

Twenty minutes later, the intercom phone in the detective bureau rang. Smoky, who was just getting ready to go home himself, listened incredulously to what the dispatcher told him, and then he grabbed his car keys and ran.

He got to the house just in time to see the ambulance lights receding in the distance, carrying Cynthia Barnett to the emergency room. The house was unbelievable, especially in comparison to how it had looked that afternoon. There was blood and scattered bits of broken glass all over the living room; in the midst of it all was the crushed body of a Persian cat.

"I don't understand," Barnett said to Smoky, haltingly. "I don't understand—why did he kill her cat?"

"I don't know," Smoky said. "I just don't know." He looked around the room. "Tell me what you can," he said.

"When I left, she was reading. She knew what was happening tonight. She was going to wait up for me. When I got home, she was lying there—just lying there. She'd been—my God—"

"All right. We'll find out her condition from the hospital. You don't have to try to tell me that. Go on."

"Go on to what?" An open-handed gesture indicated the room. "What can I tell you? I went to try and trick a blackmailer, and while I was gone he came and tried to kill my wife."

"No, Mr. Barnett," Smoky said, "he didn't try to kill her. If he'd tried to kill her she'd be dead. Can you find someplace else to stay tonight? I'd like to have a patrolman guard this crime scene, and let Duncan process it properly in the morning. But to do that I'll have to see to it everybody including you stays out tonight."

"I'll be at the hospital. Are you through with me now? I want to go on up there."

"Sure, go ahead. I'll want to talk with you in the morning, but it'll keep."

"Smoky." In the doorway Barnett turned. "Two things. The first I meant to say this afternoon and forgot I hadn't. I wish you'd call me Dave. My friends do, and I've kind of got to thinking of you as a friend. The other, to look at her, it reminded me of how it looked when that man killed Libby. Not like your pictures, but like what I saw. Somebody hit Cynthia just the same way as she was hit, only not Cynthia's head—thank God—only—only—" The same now-familiar, open-handed gesture. "For God's sake, can't somebody tell me why he killed her cat?"

"Usually when a pet is killed, it was a family member did it," Jerry Duncan told Smoky the next morning.

"What?" Smoky said blankly. But of course it was true; he knew it just as well as Duncan did. It was just that it didn't seem to apply in this case.

" 'S truth. Usually when a pet is killed as part of a mass murder, it was a family member did it," Jerry repeated. "Because to an outsider a pet is part of the surroundings, but to a family member a pet is part of the family."

"I don't understand it though," Smoky said. "They don't have any family. Neither of them. He's an only child and his parents are dead. She was raised by a maiden aunt who's dead now too. They don't have any kids. There's not any family."

"You've got him for sure ruled out?"

"He was with me!"

Jerry looked up, fingerprint brush in hand. "Was he? How, precisely, do you have the time so well figured out?"

"He didn't do this, Jerry."

"All right. Well, I didn't say always. Just usually." He surveyed the chaos around him. "Look," he said, "would you get Chuck or Linn or somebody to help me up here? It'll take me till this time tomorrow, by myself."

"Yeah, I'll get you somebody." Smoky left, taking with him the uniform man who had been detailed to guard the crime scene.

Charles Harrison, who had been chased out of bed at 4 A.M. by a sleepy and not-very-sympathetic spouse, had been sitting at the airport since five. He wanted a bathroom, some orange juice, and to go back to bed. In that order.

The key was still in sight when he took his position, just where Tommy had left it at midnight.

The coffee shop at the Mound County Airport is not a much-frequented spot, and the front booth is not popular. It was after nine o'clock before anyone sat at it.

The man who sat down didn't look at a menu. He just spoke to the waitress. As she went after the coffeepot, he picked up the key and turned it over in his hand, looking at it.

Charles got up and walked to the cashier's counter, elaborately casual, and bought a package of gum. He leaned on the counter, opening the gum, and watched the waitress pouring the coffee. He saw the man hold the key out to her, heard him say, "This was in my seat. I don't know what it is."

She looked at it. "Some sorta key, I guess," she said. "I'll put it on the counter. Maybe somebody will claim it."

She dropped it by the bowl of mints. "Whatcha got there?" Charles asked, and looked at it.

It wasn't a key.

It was a key blank.

He headed for the phone, to call Smoky.

*   *   *

The coffee shop manager and the airport manager were vehement. Nobody could have got in the coffee shop after it closed at eleven.

Nobody could have got in there during the night, to switch keys.

But the locker was empty, all the same.

VI

THE MORE SMOKY thought, the less he liked the direction his thoughts were leading him. It was perfectly true, as Jerry said, that when a pet is killed in an assault on its owner, usually the crime was committed by a member of the family. That is not a thing every cop knows. It is a thing most experienced homicide cops know.

But it was also a fact that Cynthia Barnett had no family but David Barnett.

For the rest of it, there was nothing but Barnett's word. All Smoky had really seen was a Xerox copy of an old clipping Barnett could easily have kept over the years, marked by highly disguised printing. That, and the fact that Barnett had been right about the Bonner woman being slashed after her death; the autopsy report, also in the case jacket, agreed on that.

But there was more than one way that could have happened. It did not have to be the way Barnett said it was.

That didn't make sense, though. The man was in the middle of a political campaign he badly wanted to win. If she'd been killed, maybe—but she hadn't been; she could open her eyes any moment and say who attacked her. Or could she?

The Farmer's Mound Police Department possesses only two policewomen. They would both be getting a lot of overtime for a few days, because Smoky had just made up his mind one or the other of them was going to be in that hospital room until Cynthia Barnett either woke up or died.

No need, of course, to tell him why. Just say it was for her protection.

Which, of course, it was.

The streets that made up Autumn Hill were still there; they had not been bodily removed from the city; but the activity that had once made Autumn Hill a by-word had moved to other parts of town. Some of the same houses were there, but if they'd been slums in 1941 they were doubly so now. Smoky wondered if he could locate the house Libby Bonner died in. He didn't know quite what it could tell him if he could, but—

It was still standing. It was vacant now, a For Rent sign stuck in the weeds and bare dirt of the front yard. The front door was locked but the back was half open, and Smoky walked in.

A damp, musty odor. Not really a bad smell, just an earthy one, as if the house was trying to crumble away into a mound of dirt.

The back door opened onto a little hall. To his left, the open doors of a pantry, shelves empty of all except a few fruit jars and sealing rings. To his right, the kitchen. The cabinets all seemed to be sagging, and the line where the walls and ceiling met also was unsteady. There did not seem to be one truly straight line in the place.

The kitchen was huge. It must have been enormous for one woman living alone, and the Libby Bonners of the world don't do much cooking. Fourteen-foot ceilings. No wonder the place was vacant. The way utilities were up, people who could afford no better living place than this could not afford to heat it.

Another big room. Probably meant as a dining room when the place was built, but judging from the type of debris on the floor, the last people to live here apparently had used it as a bedroom.

No telling what Libby Bonner had used it for.

That room opened, to the left, onto a little service porch, and off the service porch was a very much afterthought bathroom, consisting of a shower, toilet, and little washstand. The floor was partially rotted out now, and in places cracks were so wide he could see the ground. He wondered what it had been like then. The boy Davey Barnett would have come in here, if his story was true. For that matter, he probably came in here even if it wasn't.

To the right, the room opened onto a bedroom—a very awkward living arrangement, Smoky thought, almost as if a carpenter working without blueprints had just thrown up a wall wherever it suited his fancy.

But outside the bedroom window there was a riot of honeysuckle and rambling rose. At one time somebody who lived here had cared.

The whole front of the house was a living room, short from front to back and ridiculously wide, so that a couch would have to go on the front or back wall. The right side wall was completely filled with a large brick fireplace. A gas pipe sticking up the middle of it led to a radiant heater with most of the elements broken.

Smoky walked back through the house, this time imagining that twelve-year-old delivery boy forty-two years ago. He'd come in the kitchen door—he'd come this way—the wooden floor area in the front part of the (apparent) dining room was very badly stained. It took very little imagination to see the stains as blood.

He pulled the photographs out of the old case jacket he'd brought along.

Yes, of course. She had used this for her living room. This was where the couch had stood, facing the front of the house, with its back to the kitchen doorway, partly blocking the boy's view. There was where her body had finally been left after the slashing, midway between the couch and the door to the front room. Here, almost where Smoky was standing, must have been where the unknown assailant was standing—assuming the boy was telling the truth (the boy who was now a man, who was now a politician). Yes, here at his feet was a second dark stain. Not a large stain though. If the man had fallen this way—and the old stains in the wood seemed to say he had—then the boy would have had to step over him to get to the washstand, if he was still here when the boy went to the washstand. That, the boy would surely remember, even forty-two years later.

So whatever had happened, there was no man lying on the floor when the boy came back. If the boy came back.

Where would he have been hiding, then? Because hiding he had to have been, to come back after the boy had left the second time, to mutilate what was by then a corpse. If it was true. If it was true.

Blood stains wood, badly, and no telling how long the blood had stayed in this house before anyone made any effort to scrub it up. But forty-two years . . . spots on the floor could be pet stains, or ammonia burns where somebody left a diaper on the floor, or—or almost anything. But he knew, now, by comparing the room with the pictures, how the floor looked in the places where he knew blood had been spilled. So look for more spots like that.

There. Inside the bedroom, against an inner wall. It had spattered here, not puddled. He maybe, by that time, would have grabbed up something to try to control the bleeding. Not much blood, here. Had he maybe dashed into hiding when he heard the door open, and come back out after the boy had left to expend the rest of his rage?

Would those investigators in 1941 have missed that?

They might have, if they weren't looking for it. Unknown factors, all of them, now. There was not one name that Smoky had ever heard signed to any of the reports, and he'd been on the Farmer's Mound Police Department eleven years. Unknown how good they were, as investigators. There'd only been twelve men on the force then, but one of them either had been a good photographer or known a good photographer, because these pictures said a lot.

Of course, forty-two years. Some kid could have had a nosebleed in the bedroom ten years later.

He couldn't tell, from the report, if those investigators

had even looked in the bedroom. He guessed they had. He hoped they had.

Working a murder that is forty-two years old is a near impossibility. But somehow Smoky was sure—and maybe he was wrong, but he didn't think so—that when he knew who killed Libby Bonner he was going to know who had attacked Cynthia Barnett. And that one, he had to clear. There was certainly nothing to say Barnett was lying. But there was nothing really to say he was telling the truth, in the essential things. And sadly, it is true that when a married woman is killed (and it wasn't sure yet that Cynthia Barnett was going to live) the prime suspect is usually her husband.

He walked back down the stairs and looked out over the back yard. Shelton's Grocery was what direction—east? Yes, east. And Barnett had lived to the south. Which had he gone to, after leaving this place? He said, home. But his knife was found—wait a minute. Wait a Goddamn minute. He'd said—

"There was a big construction pit that had some water standing in it, and that's where I threw the knife, into the water. I never stopped to think that when the rain finally got over with, the knife would be visible again."

But that couldn't be true. In a week of water the knife would have rusted beyond recognition, and it would have taken at least a week for water as deep as he'd described to dry up. He'd said the knife was "a little rusted." But by now Smoky had seen the knife, had in fact already dispatched a patrolman to take it to the regional crime laboratory in Garland. And it wasn't rusted. It wasn't rusted at all.

Furthermore, when it was found, it was in the basement of a house that was being razed, a house in Autumn Hill that was west, not south or east, of Libby Bonner's house. What a silly, confused lie—and Barnett was both an intelligent and an educated man, why would he say something that was so patently not true?

It bothered Smoky. In his experience, when people lie,

they lie for a reason. They lie because they don't want the police to know the truth and don't realize the lie will be spotted as a lie. But why—why—why wouldn't Barnett want Smoky to know he'd gone west when he left Libby Bonner's house? What difference could it make?

In a basement. In a basement.

Suddenly Smoky wanted very much to talk to the person who had found the knife.

Keith Hollis was delighted to talk with Smoky. Having a cop buy him beer was a novel experience; more often, he said, cops put him in jail for drinking beer—too much of it. Over the beer he explained, gesturing with work-roughened hands. He said now, "Actually it was inside the wall. Me and Bert, we always kinda keep watchin', you know, because you'd be surprised how much stuff does turn up inside walls. Seems like people make little hidey-holes and then die, or forget about them. If it's real valuable, like jewelry or family papers, the boss tries to find out who it belongs to, but most stuff he just lets me and Bert keep. So anyways, we pulled down this section of Sheetrock wall and that knife was down inside it."

"Why'd you call the newspaper?"

"We seed the name on the knife, and Bert—you know Bert, he's cullud, and he thought it would be nice to give it back, but then I said it would be kinda fun to let the newspaper write a story about it. You know, my granddaughter, she's on the newspaper, and I know she likes that kinda thing."

Smoky took another swallow from the can, glad he'd officially gotten off duty fifteen minutes ago so he could have a beer too. "Could it maybe have been pitched in a window, to land where you found it?"

"No way. Unless somebody moved it."

Unless somebody moved it. Very much the unknown factor. Somebody could have moved it, except in that case how did it get out of the water?

"Thanks," he said, and finished his beer, only half hearing Hollis telling him the kind of funny things he'd found in the walls of other houses, older houses. He guessed the next thing to do would be to find out who had lived in that house when the knife went missing.

The library might have a 1941 city directory. It did. Everett Larsen had lived there in 1941. He also, said the long row of directories, lived there in 1940 and 1942. He went on living there until 1956, when he moved to 1502 Edison Drive. The current city directory said he was still living at 1502 Edison Drive.

Smoky drove out to 1502 Edison Drive.

Larsen was, he told Smoky, sixty-five years old "and as healthy as when I was twenty-five." Smoky had to agree he did look healthy. His white hair was thick and wavy; his stomach was flat and his arms in the white tee-shirt were muscular. He was in his back yard building a sailboat; he suspended work and offered Smoky a glass of lemonade.

Smoky wasn't too sure how well beer and lemonade would mix in his stomach but he guessed he'd take the chance. "I remember the murder, o' course," Larsen told Smoky. "Didn't like it atall, living that close to Autumn Hill, but I was a brakeman for the Texas Pacific and in them days, that was all I could afford." He looked out over the back yard, with its flowers and its garden. "Things had gotten to be different, time I retired, o' course. But—about the knife—" He shook his head. "I'm sorry, but I just don't remember finding no knife. I sure wouldn't have been hanging around by any construction pit, and if I had found one somewheres else I'd remember it. I wasn't going nowhere then, except to work; I was—I built me a lot of my own furniture, you see, and that was taking up all my spare time. I was using the basement for my workshop, and I had my tools—I had me a bench saw down there, and a big work table, and—look, I remember I wanted a good sharp knife."

"Yeah?" Smoky said encouragingly.

"I caught me a big catfish," he explained. "Forty-four pounds it was, in July of forty-one, the biggest damn fish I ever caught in my life, and I needed—look, you know what devils a catfish is to skin, and I was needing a really good knife. I remember I borrowed one from a neighbor, and I put—" Even so many years later, he began to chuckle at the memory. "I put the catfish's tail in a vise and started in with the knife and the skin was just like wet leather and the damn fish slipped outta the vise and fell on the floor and I got it back and there I was with its tail in the vise and Karen trying to hold onto the end of the tail that was at the other end of the vise and her with gloves on and me at the front end of the fish with that damn borrowed knife."

"Borrowed?" Smoky's interest, which had begun to flag, suddenly picked up. "Who did you borrow it from?"

"I don't—" Larsen frowned. "You know I don't remember now? Seems like one of the neighbors was out front when I was getting the fish out of the truck and said did I need a good knife to skin it with. And—and—I don't remember ever taking the knife back. Come to think of it, I know I didn't. Because I skinned the fish that night and then the caller called me out at three A.M. on account of the brakeman that was s'posed to have that run took sick, and then when I got back home my wife said the guy I borrowed the knife from had moved away kinda suddenlike. But anyhow, that's the only knife I can think of that wasn't just one I bought. Think it might be the one you mean?"

"It might. Can you remember what it looked like?"

"Well, it was a real good knife." He chuckled. "That don't help much, does it? It had like a bone or mother-of-pearl handle, but it wasn't one of those dull stainless steel things you get sometimes that come with the pretty handles. It had a good carbon steel blade. It cut through that ol' catfish skin real easy, once I got the catfish to hold still."

"Did it have any carving on it? Like maybe names or dates?"

"I don't remember," Larsen said. "Lord, man, that's been so many years ago. I remember about the fish because it was my fish, but the knife, it wasn't my knife."

"If you never gave it back, what did you do with it?" Smoky asked. The beer and lemonade were mixing just as badly as he'd feared they would, and he was beginning to want to get through talking to this man and get away from the lemonade. Though he wouldn't have minded relaxing on this cool green yard if he'd had another beer instead of lemonade—and if he hadn't had so much on his mind.

"I—yeah, I think I put it—look, let me explain. The basement wasn't finished. It had two-by-four studding but no inside walls. I was using the studding for shelves, for small stuff like cans of varnish, paint brushes, that sort of thing. Then later on I finished off the basement with Sheetrock. And I—after I used the knife, I washed it off and dried it real good—you know that's one thing about them good knives, they will rust if you let them stay damp—and then I think I put it up high on some of that studding, where the kids couldn't get at it. And then I—you understand, it's been a mighty long time ago. But I don't remember moving it. I don't ever remember touching it again, and I think if I had I would remember."

"So you think you put the Sheetrock over it."

"Yes," Larsen said. "I could have, you know. If it was up high enough that I couldn't see it."

"Do you remember where your neighbor said he got it?"

"If I remembered that," Larsen said, "I'd remember which neighbor it was. But you got to understand what the neighborhood was like. They got a fancy word for it now, transitional, but we had them then. People mostly didn't stay long, and sometimes they were white and sometimes they were cullud. It would have been white, because in those days we didn't mix much, but I can't remember anything else." He stood up. "Karen might know. Just a minute." He went toward the back door.

Smoky looked around at the yard. It was quiet here, and as tired as Kathy's nocturnal howling was leaving him, he could very easily go to sleep in this chair. By clock time it was five o'clock, but the sun said it was just past four. The clouds were high and fleecy and here, on this lawn, the breeze was cool.

Larsen came back. "She don't know either. She said she can think of five neighbors we had in forty-one that moved all of a sudden."

Karen Larsen came out the kitchen door behind her husband, as stout as he was slim, with a homely smell of yeast and buttermilk on her. "I don't remember who lived where when," she said. "I know they was Toby Greer, he lived nearby about four months, had him a wife and three kids, and I guess they moved away 'cause the house was just too little. Then there was, oh, I don't remember his name, hers was Mary Elliot. He was a butcher, I recall, and she was kind of stupid. Borrowed my toaster 'cause she didn't know how to make toast in the oven and then ruined it trying to make buttered toast in it. They just up and moved away in the middle of the night. Then they was George Revills. He played in one of them bands, so he would come and go a good bit. He wasn't married, and he kept having that kind of party that allus wound up with people having fights in the yard, so's I had to call the law on him a couple of times. Of course, Kevin Verner, he moved away kind of sudden, but he'd lived there a good long time. He was a city policeman couple of years, but him and his wife, they just couldn't get along noway, and when she moved out he stayed a few more months and then he moved away too. And then they was Bill Hammersmith, he was a construction worker, and you know them construction workers, they do move around a lot. He stayed around four months and I think Esther said he left some rent owing her when he left."

A construction worker. A construction pit. Very possibly he had just been given the explanation of how the knife got in the house where it was found. Bill Hammersmith found it and took it home, loaned it to Everett Larsen, and Larsen used it, set it on a two-by-four and forgot it and later put a wall around it.

In which case Barnett wasn't lying. Smoky felt slightly cheered, and wondered how he'd go about looking for Bill Hammersmith. He hadn't the slightest idea where to start, and it probably wouldn't be worth the trouble to find him. He wondered if Karen Larsen had that encyclopedic a memory of everybody she'd ever met. He suspected she did.

Steven Simons was busy with the Rangers again. He'd invited them to dinner, and presumably Melissa and Tommy were taking care of the meal. Simons was seeing to it warrants were in order.

From what they had determined from the women they'd talked to, the man would do the job in either his home or theirs, depending on their preference, although they had indicated that for the past six months he'd shown a definite preference for his own home. Melissa would be going there. Presumably he'd be ready for her.

The police planned to be ready for him. That readiness meant the small electronic bugging device to fit in Melissa's purse, an arrest warrant, and a search warrant. On the search warrant were listed all the items to be seized: the speculums, the scalpels, the suction devices, the drugs (the women all insisted he had everything, just like a regular doctor; and two of their witnesses were dopers and knew their drugs. Those two specified morphine and Demerol).

The arrest warrant was based on the word of the one woman who'd promised to testify about her abortion last October. A bitterly angry woman, Maria Coody, not at George Revills but at her mother. She hadn't wanted the abortion, but her mother had insisted she get it, and had ruled out any legal clinics for fear of publicity. She'd used tampons after it. Revills told her not to, she said, but she couldn't see why it would matter, and she hadn't gone to the doctor until her temperature was 106 degrees. Maria would never have a child now.

And yet, all of this careful preparation really amounted to no more than an excuse. They really weren't extremely interested in charging him with performing a legal operation on a willing person in an illegal manner, and blaming him for Maria's hysterectomy would be a long way from first causes. But they wanted a reason for a legal arrest, so that they could talk with him, question him, and, they hoped, find out whether he was indeed the man who had impregnated, aborted, and killed a fourteen-year-old girl with the mind of a four-year-old.

Simons felt his coat pocket to be sure he had picked up the transmitter as well as the warrants. Then he stood up. "Ready for supper?" he asked the Rangers.

"You sure your daughter won't mind us dropping in like this?"

"She knows we're coming," Simons answered. "Taking your own car? I'll be in the white Plymouth, then; just follow me out."

"It's cheating to buy potato salad," Melissa said.

"Not if you really didn't have time to make it," Tommy assured her. "Anyway, you added the celery and sweet pickles to it, so it's not like it was just bought. Hey, that's good barbecue sauce."

"Keep your hands out of it," Melissa scolded. "Dog-gone you, Tommy, quit it! That's for supper!"

" 'S good, though," he said, his mouth full. He swallowed. "I didn't have time to eat lunch today. Not to finish it, anyway. I started but we had to leave in the middle because we had a call to a signal seven."

"Yeah?" Melissa, easily translating that to disorderly conduct, paused in the act of pouring barbecue sauce on the steaks. "Where was it?"

94

"Oh, just a bar. We got there and these two dudes was fighting over some broad."

"It's not nice to call a woman a broad."

"But she really was a broad. I mean she was five ax handles and a plug of chewing tobacco across the rump."

"You're kidding."

"Uh-uh. I don't know how big five ax handles are really, that's just what Charles said, but it was the biggest damn woman I ever saw in my life."

"Black or white?"

"White. It was that little ol' bar next door to the Holt Hotel." She nodded. The Holt Hotel is where Farmer's Mound's small population of winos and drifters tends to gather. "Anyhow," he continued, "these two dudes were just a-swinging over her, and both of them was so drunk they couldn't see where they were hitting. We jailed them both for disorderly. But when we got that taken care of we had a dog call and then we had a juvenile signal seven over by Carver High School and what with one thing and another we just never did get through with lunch."

"Who was fighting who at Carver?"

"It was two white kids in a fight because one of them said the other one had stolen the first one's bicycle and then their friends got in it and then one of them pulled out a little .22 pistol."

"Oh," she said, and tried to shrug. "Well, it could have been worse. It could have been a shotgun." She abandoned the salad she was making and came to his arms, and he knew she was thinking about yesterday, about the solid slugs spinning the police car in circles in the street.

"I'm okay, Melissa," he told her. "You want to know something? I'm damn scared about this thing you're going on tonight."

"I am too, a little. But it'll all be okay."

"Sure it will." He let go of her. "Come on, let's go check the charcoal." A minute later he said, "I hope those Rangers hurry up. This fire is ready for the steaks."

*   *   *

95

The Rangers were named Mike and Jim, and they were both young men. Their captain, who'd helped with the planning, had been called back to his office, but they were sure they could take care of everything. They had about them the hard young arrogance of men who can shoot in the high nineties and haven't yet been stomped in a street fight. Tommy, who also shot in the nineties but was still hurting some in the ribs, regarded them with some wariness.

The steaks were a wasted effort. But after a pretense of eating, Steve produced the transmitter. It had been wrapped in a cigarette package, the top fourths of most of the package of extra-long cigarettes neatly placed back on top of it. "Lissa," he said, "go to your room and put this thing in your purse and start talking. You can't hear us, but we'll be hearing you. We need to get a range on it. Tommy, this is the receiver. When she starts talking, you walk down the street. See how far away you can get and still hear her clearly. Here." He handed him a police walkie-talkie set on tach three, which by rule was never used except on special details. "Let me know how far you get."

The transmitter carried three blocks before it started to cut out. "That'll do," Simons said. "We won't be anything like that far away." He looked at his watch. "It's that time. You ready, young'un?"

"I guess." She looked uncertainly at Tommy.

"Okay. Mike will take you up there. We'll be covering the doors. Remember, if we can't hear you, or if you have any kind of trouble at all, we'll be right there."

"Okay," Melissa said, and looked again at Tommy. Then she got in the car with the Ranger.

"You're kinda crazy about that guy, aren't you, girl?" he asked.

"Yes, I guess I am. Isn't that the way it usually is?" she asked, staring intently at a white bird strutting long-leggedly through a field of cattle.

"No," Mike said, "if it was, a bastard like this one would be out of work. You scared?"

"A little."

"You should be. Anybody that's not scared when it's time to be is a damn fool and I wouldn't have him for a partner." He looked in his rearview mirror at the white Plymouth just cresting a hill behind them. "But that man of yours, he doesn't seem to me like he scares easy."

"He scares," Melissa said. "But not easy." She shivered. "I wish he did scare a little easier."

The Ranger glanced at her. "You gonna make him quit?"

"Make him quit what?"

"Policing. You gonna make him quit policing?"

"No. I don't think I could anyway. But if I could it wouldn't be fair. He likes policing."

The car stopped. "This is the place, girl. You got your story straight?"

"Yes." She got out of the car and carefully shut the door. After she shut it, the car headed back the way it came for half a block, and then stopped on the side of the road where Mike turned on his borrowed city police walkie-talkie. The other three men, together behind the house, had the receiver to Melissa's transmitter, and they'd keep him posted. He lit a cigarette. He guessed he'd have time for one. Maybe two.

"I'm—I'm Melissa," she stammered, to the man who had opened the door. "They told me—Mike told me—to come here." She wasn't just a little scared now. She was terrified.

"Come in." He wasn't what she had expected. He might have killed Rosemary, but he didn't look like a man who would hurt Rosemary. He was tall and she guessed he must be in his sixties, but he was a tidy-looking man, clean-shaven, and he wore a nice aftershave. "Sit down," he told her.

The room didn't look like Texas. The front of the house was Texas, with a bad lawn of Bermuda grass, but inside—this had been a living room but there'd been work done to it—there were hundreds of books on floor-to-ceiling shelves, a sort of combined desk and room divider, a black spinet, an oriental-looking coffee table with a bowl of flowers on it, and two Queen Anne chairs beside it. Except for the desk chair and the piano bench, there was no other seating in the room. He sat down beside her in the second chair. "You understand why Mike brought you here?"

"It's—it's for an abortion. Because I c-c-can't—I can't—"

"You can't have the baby?"

"I can't—I can't—I don't know how to tell my daddy," she got out. And that had been true; she had wept to Tommy after she left the doctor's office, saying, "I can't tell Daddy, I don't know how to tell Daddy," and the crying stopped only when Tommy promised her that was a task he would take.

And then he'd said, "I've got to go, Lissa, I'm not even supposed to be here, it's off my beat," and he'd promised her he'd go to the house as soon as he got off work and talk to Simons. And then he'd walked back down the dirt alley to where he'd parked the black and white.

"All right," the man was saying. "You can't have the baby, and you can't tell your father. What does your mother think?"

"My mother's dead."

"Well." The man stood up. ' You understand I have to charge a higher fee than a normal clinic would? Everything I use must be obtained secretly, and the expense to me is high."

"I brought the money." Nothing so obvious as marked bills. Just bills with the serial numbers recorded, photographed. Five hundred dollars belonging to the state of Texas.

"This way." Over his shoulder he said, "It is fortunate

you were willing to come here. It is much easier for me to control sterility here than elsewhere. But some women, particularly older women, prefer that I go to their homes."

"Will it hurt?"

"Some discomfort is inevitable, but I try to keep it at a minimum."

"This looks like a regular operating room."

"I do what I can to ensure safety." He looked around complacently. "Before we continue, are you in fact certain of pregnancy? You're quite young. Sometimes a woman of your age will have certain—ah—irregularities if she is extremely frightened of the possibility."

If I wanted this, Melissa thought, if this is what I wanted, he'd be soothing me with this kind of talk. "I'm sure," she heard herself saying. "My doctor—there were tests—"

"Before you disrobe let me check—yes. Just below the pelvic bone—eight weeks?"

"Seven."

"A little advanced then. Well. I will leave the room to allow you to disrobe. There is a gown on the table there; just slip it on."

Tommy, listening, came to his feet. "No longer. I won't wait any longer."

"Then let's hit it." Simons spoke into the walkie-talkie.

As they went toward the house, they could hear Revills ask, "You aren't prepared?"

"I—I'm scared. Let me think a minute—"

"My poor child," the man said, "surely you won't let a moment's fear now cause you to bear this unwanted burden. Your blouse opens at the back? Here, let me help you—"

Tommy's strides lengthened. He didn't pause at the back door; he hit it with his shoulder and kept on going. Down the hall he could hear Melissa saying, "Don't—" and then he hit that door.

"Freeze, you son of a bitch!" he shouted. "You're

under arrest! Melissa, get behind me."

Melissa walked around the table, staying well out of the man's reach. George Revills very prudently put his hands in the air. "Well, well, well!" he said. "It's been years since I was arrested. And by such an impetuous young officer! Are you by any chance Mike?"

"Mike is a Ranger. I'm Officer Inman, Farmer's Mound Police Department."

"So, Officer Inman, I'm under arrest. Are you perchance the father of the baby the young lady is expecting? Because she really is pregnant, you know."

"Yes, I am."

"And you have not yet seen fit to—ah—endow her with a ring? I did look at her hands. I always look at their hands."

"I can't see that that's any concern of yours," Tommy said stiffly. "I can assure you the matter is under control."

"Then why did she come to me?"

"Because we told her to," Simons said, in the hall. He came into the room. "We'll take over here, son. You better take Melissa on home." Tommy, going toward her, heard Simons behind him droning, "You have the right to remain silent—"

VII

"I DON'T WANT a lawyer just now," Revills said. "Maybe later. Is that a search warrant? Do you mind if I read it over? I've never seen one before. And a Ranger, how fascinating, that's something else I never saw before. Somehow I fancied Rangers all wore grey Stetsons and cowboy boots."

"Only on parade," one of the Rangers told him.

"Why don't you park yourself and read the warrant?" Simons said. "That copy is yours anyway. And I just feel sure we're going to be here awhile."

Revills was looking over the list of items sought. "All of it is in this room, of course, except the ledger," he said, "but I suppose you'll insist on searching the rest of the house too, no matter what I say. Dear me, do you plan to haul away all my surgical equipment? You'll need a truck."

"We weren't expecting this much," Simons admitted, looking around. Melissa's exclamation had been no exaggeration. What had been one bedroom of the house was now a rather fully equipped operating room, complete with extremely large and bright overhead lights and an oxygen tank. "Where did you get all this?"

"You can buy some really interesting things military surplus," Revills said, "if you shop carefully. As to the rest of it, well, say I had connections and leave it at that. This isn't really much. I haven't been back in Farmer's Mound quite a year, and I'm retired except for just keeping my hand in now and then. You should have seen what I had in my old home, now that was complete. But I had some of my equipment taken out of storage and sent down here a few months after I moved, for the benefit of a lady who—ah—preferred to vacation in Texas. Reputation, you see. The lady's husband is rather active in politics in another state, and with political considerations in mind she felt it unlikely she would feel comfortable at even the most exclusive and private of abortion clinics."

Simons didn't particularly care who the woman in question was. One of the Rangers, who had been examining the contents of several metal cabinets in the room, now turned and said, "I think we'd better send for that truck he mentioned."

"You'll be wanting to talk with me, Captain," Revills said. "Would you mind if we at least begin our discussion in my study? I realize you'll want to take me downtown later, but you might be interested in asking questions about things that turn up in the course of your search."

With a rather bewildered feeling that the arrest had been taken out of his hands by the prisoner, Captain Simons followed Revills into the room Melissa had first entered. Revills reached for a desk drawer and stopped abruptly. "Would you prefer to open it yourself?"

"Go ahead," Simons told him. "I'm watching you." He was; this didn't seem like the type of person likely to start a ruckus, but sometimes the most unlikely people did exactly that.

What Revills took out of the drawer was a sealed-in-cellophane box labelled "Scotch Brand 120 Minutes High Performance." He opened the box, tossing cellophane into a wastebasket, and put the tape cassette into a recorder. "Now," he said, seating himself, "shall we begin?"

With some unwilling admiration for the man, Simons replied, "Since we're taping it, why don't I begin my repeating some of what I've already told you? My name is Steven Simons. I'm a detective captain with the Farmer's Mound Police Department. You are being charged with criminal abortion and practicing medicine without a license, and you are under investigation for other matters. You have the right to remain silent. . . . Do you understand all this, and do you wish to give up the right to remain silent?"

"My name is George Revills," the man said quite formally, his voice holding only the slightest hint that he was putting on a performance. "I do understand these rights as they have been explained to me. I wish to waive the right to remain silent at this time. I am making this statement quite voluntarily and I will contact my attorney when I want to. Are you hunting my ledger, young man? It's in the next drawer down, but you won't understand it without my key, which is not located in your jurisdiction. Now—" He returned to Captain Simons. "Where shall I begin?"

"Wherever you want to. We can get on to specific questions later."

"Wherever I want to. God, that covers a lot of territory." He seemed to unbend slightly. "I'm sixty-six years old. How old are you, Captain?"

"Forty-one."

"Forty-one. Do you have any grandchildren? No, not yet, I suppose."

"Give me time. Melissa is my daughter."

"Oh, I see." A mirthless smile. "Keeping the policing in the family. I had one granddaughter. She's dead. My daughter won't give me houseroom. She disapproves of my profession. It sent her to good schools, but she's ashamed of the source of the money." He leaned back in the chair. "All right. The beginning. I was—a musician, of sorts. That sounds romantic, doesn't it? A musician in the Big Band Era. No, perhaps not, to you. You aren't old enough to remember the Big Band Era. We had a lot of one-night stands, and we made enough money to eat and dress not well, but flashy, and to get from booking to booking. When we didn't have any bookings I came home to Farmer's Mound. I lived in Autumn Hill in those days.

You're young, but you're a cop. Do you know what Autumn Hill was like in those days?"

"I've heard stories," Simons admitted softly. A direct question needed a response, but just now he didn't want to interrupt the chain of thought.

"There was a girl I cared a lot about. She wasn't from Farmer's Mound; she lived in Dallas, but we travelled together. In those days things weren't free and easy the way they are now. Even in the entertainment world where things were always looser, an illegitimate baby was a disaster that could mark the end of everything. The girl—I don't know whose baby it was, by the way; it certainly wasn't mine. But she tried to abort it. With a coat hanger, in a hotel room. She nearly bled to death before someone found her. They did a hysterectomy but she died a week later of septicemia."

Simons nodded, and Revills went on, "I decided, then, I was going to be an abortionist. Only I was going to be a good one. I've been. I've been. I've done, I don't know, probably several thousand, and I've only lost one patient. I made money, in that and other things too, but that wasn't why I did it—I did some free ones too. Only one death, that's a pretty good record, wouldn't you say? You wonder why I'm telling you this?" He smiled, faintly. "The times have changed. The world doesn't need me anymore. The scared little girls don't have to use coat hangers in hotel rooms anymore. Your daughter put on a very convincing act, by the way."

"My daughter was scared. She wants her baby. And she loved Rosemary."

"*Rosemary*?" There was naked shock in the man's voice. "Is that the reason for this masquerade? You thought I was it on Rosemary?"

"We have witnesses that have seen you with her many times, but her mother insists she doesn't know you. And you do have a record for child molestation as well as abortion."

"Oh, yes, you would have witnesses, and it is true her mother doesn't know me now. Rosemary was my granddaughter. Though if I had known she needed aborting I assure you she would be alive now. As to that child molestation charge—" He shook his head. "That's really an old one. I knew the girl was—in the phrase of the time—jailbait. But she appeared to be at least sixteen. No one could have seen her and guessed she was twelve, until they took her into court in a loose dress and braids and no makeup. But . . . Rosemary? No. Not Rosemary."

And probably he was telling the truth. All that would be too easily disproved for him to lie about it. "Where did you get your training?" Simons asked.

"The navy," the man said blandly. "Oh, they didn't know that was what they were teaching me, I assure you. It wasn't in the curriculum. But first I became a hospital corpsman, and then I managed to get sent to another school to become an operating-room technician. Then I managed to get assigned to the ob-gyn clinic in a rather large naval hospital. It is really," he said, "gratifying what a person can learn, when he sets his mind to it. And even in the navy there was always a doctor or two—you understand that, of course."

Simons agreed he understood that.

"Then after the war was over and I was discharged I set about finding customers. I knew what I was doing. And I —as I said, I had connections, even at first. I was in business for over thirty years, with this and other things, and then I retired last year—bad health—and moved back home. I've done a few jobs here but not many, and I'd always done an occasional one here, when I happened to be home, for old friends. But as I said, I'm not really needed anymore."

A long shot, Simons thought. "How about Mary Thomas? Did you know her?"

"Past tense on her, too? Yes, I knew Mary. I aborted her twice. She was a friend of a friend. I never made any money on her, it was just, I was sorry for her. Like my little singer in 1940, she was so stupid and so scared. But the second time I nearly lost her, had a hard time getting the bleeding stopped, and I told her then she better get on the Pill or get her tubes tied. She came to me about a month ago, four months gone which is farther along than I handle anyway, and I told her no and I told her to go to a doctor. And why do you ask about Mary Thomas—though I guess I have a pretty good idea."

"She was found dead of an abortion, not far from here."

"Not one of mine. No. Not one of mine."

And Steve Simons, who had seen the body of Mary Thomas and now had seen George Revills's operating room, was very much inclined to believe him. "No, I don't expect it was. But as a matter of curiosity, would you mind telling me what you did with the body of the one you did lose? You realize you don't have to, of course."

"Well, as I suppose it is technically murder, I think I would prefer not to tell you the city and state, except to say that it was not here and it was not in my—ah—customary locale. But I deposited the body, in approved fashion, in the emergency-room parking lot at the nearest hospital. And then I—ah—cut and ran."

One of the Rangers came back in. "Captain Simons, may I see you for a minute?" He glanced at the tape recorder.

"Sure thing." Simons stepped back out into the hall. "Yeah, Jim?"

"Look, there's no sense in us trying to move this stuff tonight," Jim said. "He's right, it *would* take a truck. I just called the head of the state crime lab and he wants to fly in tomorrow and have a look. What say we post a uniform man here for now and get at it again tomorrow?"

"I've got no problem with that," Simons answered. He looked back toward Revills. "I'll take him on down to the station, but unless I miss my guess he'll lose no time making bond."

"Well, he'll just have to stay out of here, that's all."

If anybody had accused Smoky O'Donnell of being a dedicated police officer, he would have denied it. Furthermore, he would have said he didn't know any dedicated police officers. A dedicated police officer, he would have said, is just somebody who doesn't know when to go home. If questioned further, however, he would have had to admit to being the kind of police officer who doesn't know when to go home.

Except on this night he had gone home. He had gone home exactly long enough to eat supper and assist in putting the boy to bed, but then he had come back up to the office. Not that he was doing anything at the moment that particularly demanded night work, but there was always work he could do. Besides, he was restless and didn't want to disturb Audra. Kathy had finally learned to sleep a few hours at a time, and Audra was slowly beginning to catch up on her sleep. Smoky figured he'd stay home more when Audra was rested.

He looked up from the intelligence file he was working on when Captain Simons came in. The file could wait; it wasn't extremely pushing. Things were beginning to fit together in it, and he expected that within the next month this particular person was going to be the subject of a very carefully timed raid, but just at the moment there was nothing urgent about it. "Who have you got there?" he asked, recognizing the Rangers but not the person in handcuffs. This looked like a rather unlikely person to be handcuffed anyway, but the Farmer's Mound Police Department has a rule. All prisoners are transported in handcuffs.

"This is George Revills," Simons said. "We're charging

him with abortion." He wasn't expecting the reaction he got.

"Revills? *Revills?*" The name clearly meant something to Smoky. "Well, well, well! George Revills. You lived in Autumn Hill in nineteen forty-one, didn't you?"

"I did," Revills said, not appearing to be surprised that this unknown small blond man knew his background that well.

"You moved away from there rather suddenly, didn't you?"

"I did," Revills agreed. "As I recall, I left about two months of rent unpaid. Did you want to discuss that?"

"I haven't the least interest in your rent. I would, however, like to ask you about a girl named Libby Bonner."

"I didn't know a Libby Bonner." But his eyes said he did, and Simons was bewildered at the turn this was taking. He didn't know a Libby Bonner either.

"Steve," Smoky said, "could we put him back there in an interview room and let me talk to you?"

"Yeah, sure," answered Simons, still looking bewildered. "Mr. Revills, back there, please, and shut the door."

Simons listened as Smoky told him in some detail what he'd been working on. "But Smoky," he pointed out, "Revills isn't an especially tall man. And a scar like that would show."

"We don't know how short Barnett might have been when he was twelve years old," Smoky argued. "And we really don't know how deep a cut we're talking about."

"So you're suspecting him, maybe, of the attack on Cynthia Barnett? I don't think so, Smoky. But it wouldn't hurt to get Barnett to look at him, I guess, if he's as sure as you think he is that he'd recognize him. I don't see how he could."

"I don't know if he could," Smoky said. "But—" He looked meditatively at the closed door to the interview room. "It's worth a try."

A person cannot refuse to take part in a lineup. But he does have the right to have an attorney present at the lineup, in order to see that the lineup is conducted fairly and not in a way that will single out one person as different from all the others. With this fact explained to him, George Revills looked at the rights-to-a-lineup waiver form in front of him, one sheet of mimeographed paper. "I guess I don't mind signing that," he said, "because I don't need an attorney present to have somebody say I'm not the right person. And I'm not." He scratched his head. "But I hope you're not planning on having a lineup right now. Because it's nearly midnight. And I'm an old man. I would like to get some sleep, even if it is in jail."

Simons didn't, these days, think of sixty-six as old, but he said, "No, I don't want to hold it tonight, unless you want to get bonded out tonight."

"No," Revills said. "I don't. You want to know something? I really don't care. Not anymore."

After he was taken up to jail, Simons turned. "Smoky," he said, "he didn't do it, you know. Not that."

"No, I don't think he did, now," Smoky said. "But I'd still like to be sure."

"Be sure in the morning," Simons said. "I'm going home."

Seconds later the telephone rang, and Smoky reached for it. "Detective Bureau, O'Donnell speaking."

"Who put this guard on my wife?"

"Huh? Barnett? I did."

"Well, I appreciate it and all that, but they won't leave even for me, and that I don't appreciate."

"They have their orders," Smoky said. "Can't we talk about it in the morning?"

"No, we can talk about it now. Who the hell gave them those orders?"

"Well, I did, as a matter of fact," Smoky said. "Look, there are reasons but it's too late to explain them now. I was just getting ready to go home, and—"

"The hell it's too late to explain them now!"

So he explained.

The suddenly very quiet voice at the other end of the line said, "I see. So he was right, then, whoever he was, that he could make you think—"

"No, Mr. Barnett, he wasn't. The FBI has done a very careful study of—"

"But it's not always."

"I never said it was."

"I remember reading in the paper a few years back where there was a case in which five people and a great big dog were shot and one member of the family was left unharmed. I guess you would have said that surviving family member did it, wouldn't you?"

"At least I'd have looked at him good and hard," Smoky said, vaguely remembering the case. "And that's all—"

"But he didn't. A week later they charged a neighbor from across the street."

A neighbor. That's one thing he hadn't thought about. "Is there anybody that was your neighbor then and is again now?"

"I didn't mean—"

"But I do," Smoky said. "It's worth thinking about. Think, would you? And don't complain about the policewomen. No, we don't really think you did it, but we have to look, and no matter who did it, she needs protection from a repeat attack. You can't talk with her while she's asleep anyway, and when she wakes up we'll ask them to leave the room while you're there."

"All right. All right. I'll talk with you in the morning. I'll think about the neighbors." A soft little click.

Smoky stood up, looked at the clock which now said one, and guessed he would go home. He walked slowly around the detective bureau turning off light switches, pulled the door closed, and walked down the darkened hall past the lighted desk sergeant's office, to go on out to his own car.

"Dave Barnett is probably going to be down early this morning," Smoky told Captain Simons at seven-thirty. "He's not very happy about the guard on his wife." "No, I didn't expect he would be. But you know, Smoky, even if you had the knife explained, which you really don't, it still wouldn't explain how the briefcase got out of the locker. The only explanation I can see that makes sense is that the key wasn't left there to begin with. Maybe Tommy and Charles were sitting there keeping guard over a key blank. Maybe he didn't stay at the hospital all night. Maybe he attacked her before he left the house, and then slipped out of the hospital long enough to go back to the terminal during the night." "But why?" Smoky asked. "I'm—maybe I'm being stupid but I just can't see it. I just can't believe it. Even putting aside his personality, the roots go back too far. You don't start setting up a cover story forty-two years before you do a thing." "No. I know. I don't see it either. But I just don't see any other answer." The phone rang and Simons picked it up. "Yeah? Okay." He hung up. "Dispatch says we got a safe burglary at Trinity Finance. Nobody else is in yet." "But look, I've got—" "David Barnett coming in. I know. You've also got a safe burglary to work. I'll pacify Barnett till you get back in, and I'll send Jerry out as soon as he's here. He should be—" He picked up the work sheet. "Off today. I'll send you Linn. She's going to be a little late—oh hell. I can't send you Linn either. She's got to go relieve Kay at the hospital. I'm sorry, Smoky. Go work the burglary." "Where's Chuck?" "Out sick."

"Shit," Smoky said, and picked up the Speed Graphic case in one hand and the car keys and a walkie-talkie in the other hand and kicked the door open. There was a fingerprint kit in the car and a moulage plaster kit in the trunk.

It was, he thought, a problem at times to be a detective on a small police force in a town that was getting some large town problems, and with the result that you needed to be able to do everything.

Well, almost everything. Jerry would search any latent fingerprints he brought in and Chuck would develop the pictures he took.

Looking at Trinity Finance, he shook his head. They couldn't have made it easier for burglars if they'd tried. There was a wall, shoulder high, all around the back and both sides, liberally planted in rambler roses. So the burglar had walked in at the back driveway (located at the left back) and walked around to the right side of the building. There he had crouched down, safely out of sight of any patrol cars or curious bystanders, and gone to work.

The building was wired for a burglar alarm along the front windows and the front and back doors. But the wiring didn't extend to the walls, which were rather simply constructed of sheets of metal bolted together. Some sort of prefab building, Smoky guessed. The burglar had popped four bolts with a tire tool, pried back enough of that panel to reach in with metal shears, and then simply cut himself a little door.

Once inside he had rummaged through all the desks in the place, taking coffee money and postage stamps. Then he had turned the safe (which wasn't a safe at all, but a fire-resistant lock box) on its side and hammered out the bottom with a sledge hammer.

After which he walked away with four thousand dollars in cash which never should have been left there to start with; the lock box was clearly labelled "Not to be Used for Safe Storage of Valuables."

Smoky took pictures with the Speed Graphic and stored it back in the car. He dusted for fingerprints and lifted four good latents off the sheet metal wall. He asked questions; he made a plaster cast of a footprint by the wall, and while it was setting, he asked more questions.

Then he went back to the office and put the Speed Graphic back in the corner, the plaster cast on the floor in a cardboard box, the used film pack on Chuck's desk, and the four lifted fingerprints on Jerry's desk, properly labelled; and then he sat down at the typewriter, laid his pocket notebook on the desk, and without referring to his notebook but twice he typed out a three-page report.

"Pro job?" Simons asked.

"Semi-pro. It wasn't a beginner but it wasn't a very good safe."

"Umm," Simons said, reading the report. "And nothing to look for on the pawn sheets. You know, this kinda reminds me of that one at Texas Loan two months back. Did we ever get anybody on that one?"

"Uh-uh. But he didn't get anything either. They hadn't left but twenty-four dollars in the safe."

"That could be kinda discouraging to a burglar." Because they both knew a burglar sweated for what he got, not near as much as he would at an honest job, but enough that he wouldn't repeat a completely unprofitable one. "So if it was the same one who did it, he must have known about the cash. I wonder if they'd let us look over their list of customers."

"I'm way ahead of you," Smoky said. "And I recognized half the names on it. It's a nickel and dime outfit, you know, the kind where you borrow two hundred dollars and pay back seven-fifty a week and you aren't supposed to notice by the time you're through you've paid back three hundred and fifty-nine dollars, but they've stuck on so many hidden charges that on paper it's just eighteen percent interest."

"One of those."

"One of those, yeah." Which was what they were doing with four thousand dollars in cash. A more conventional finance company does all its business with checks.

"Barnett called," Simons said. "He'll be up about ten to see the lineup. He's still not very happy about the policewomen. He said to tell you he thought about the neighbors and can't think of any that are likely. Know what he means?"

"Yeah. Have you got the lineup set up?"

"Right." It had involved getting the jailors to wash and shave four winos, but that was the only way to arrive at five fairly similar-looking men to put in the lineup. "And I hope nothing else new comes up," Simons said, "because we are damn shorthanded. If we don't start getting some more people in here—" He shook his head.

"Know what you mean," Smoky answered. "You say Barnett'll be up in half an hour?"

VIII

Smoky was typing a report. "Composition of lineup as follows: No. 1, Joe Reno W/M 47. No. 2, George Revills W/M 66. No. 3, Allen Carson W/M 62. No. 4, Sam Stanfield W/M 55. No. 5, Carl Alexander, W/M 49. Photo of lineup taken with Polaroid is in case jacket." Despite the wide age variance, once the winos were cleaned up they looked a lot the same.

For all the good it had done. Barnett had taken one look and said, "No. It's not any of them."

They had sent the lineup back to jail and leaned on Barnett a little, quite tactfully, because even though he was in civil law rather than criminal law he was still a lawyer and knew his rights. He spotted it all the same and said, "Look, you keep asking me questions. Let *me* ask *you* one. You really think I did it, don't you? You think I killed Libby Bonner and you think I tried to kill my wife, don't you?"

"No, we don't," Smoky said.

"Then why the hell—"

"Listen to me. The truth, all right? That's what you're asking for, right? All the cards on the table? Let it all hang out? All right. We don't think you did either one of those things, but you're making it harder and harder for us to keep on thinking that, because there are some major discrepancies between what you tell us and what we know to be facts. May I tell you what they are?"

"I wish you would."

"All right. To start with, you told me you threw your knife into a construction pit full of water and went home.

When I said something about the probability that it would have been badly rusted you said something like, oh, well, the blade was rusted. Well, the blade wasn't rusted. My God, Barnett, didn't you realize I'd go and get the knife? The state crime lab has it now. And before I get to that, look here." He unfolded a city map. "Here's where Libby Bonner lived. Right here." He circled it.

"Now," he went on, "here's where you lived then. And here's where the store was. You told us you threw the knife away on the way home. If you had been on your way home you'd have taken, approximately, this route. But maybe you went back to the store first? Well, if you had here's where you'd have gone." He was tracing out routes with a pencil. "But the knife turned up in the basement of a house clear over here." He pointed.

"Now, I'll concede," he continued, "that there are several ways that could have happened. But there's more. You may not know how much a modern crime laboratory can do. Let me tell you. Stuff gets down in the cracks of a knife where the blade is joined to the hilt and it stays. The lab found two types of human blood, A and O. They also found fish blood. We know how that got there. You told us how one kind of human blood got there. We gouged up pieces of wood from the floor of that house and sent it to the lab. Whether you care to believe it or not, they could still tell things about it, even now. Where she bled—and remember, we know this from the pictures—was type A. We already knew from the autopsy reports that she was type A. Where he bled—if it was him, anyway, the second bloody area—was type O. All right. Where'd the type A blood in the knife come from? Would you care to tell me you had a nosebleed?"

"No, I wouldn't. Not that it would do any good. I'm type O too. I suppose you already knew that. Are you suggesting I did have a nosebleed and that other blood was from me? As to the A—I dropped the knife by her body, but she wasn't bleeding that much then."

116

"No, I wasn't suggesting anything and I didn't know your blood type."

"Now you do. What else?" He was breathing hard.

"The locker key. You supposedly left a locker key on the seat of the coffee shop. It was either under police surveillance or inaccessible at all times. But the next morning what was there was a key blank. And the locker was empty. How do you suppose that happened?"

"I don't know." He dropped his forehead in the palm of his hand and shook his head. "I don't know. I didn't know any of that about the knife. I don't know how her blood type got on it, and I don't know how it got where it was found, and if you know how fish blood got on it you're way ahead of me because I never cleaned fish with it. And I never bled on it and I sure as hell didn't know his blood type. Or hers for God's sake. And I don't know how the key got switched. I asked you to keep a guard there all night. Would I if I'd been going to—hell yes, I suppose I might, if I'd already switched keys. All right. All right. I see what you mean. But I've told you the truth, every damn thing I told you was true. The knife—I tried not even to look at it, even while I was washing it off. I threw it—"

He looked at the map. "I pitched it into a pit right here, where they were digging out the big holes for the gasoline storage tanks for a service station they were building. It was a Humble station then, it's an Exxon now, and I think the same guy still owns it. It might—I didn't look back. I threw it and ran. I suppose it might have caught on something and not gone all the way in. And about the key, I don't know. I don't know. My God, I don't know. I must —I suppose I must seem very unreasonable to you. I guess it does look to you like I'm lying. Maybe I should know all those answers. But I don't. I'm sorry, but I don't. Keep the guards with Cynthia. Put the Marines in there if you want to. But find out who did it. Because I don't know."

And both detectives could sense the utter weariness and

frustration in the man. "No," Simons said, "I don't think you do know. We do intend to keep the policewomen in there, because whoever he is, he might try again. Chances are we'll want to keep them in there even after she does wake up. But—look—try to remember. Because at one time you must have known something."

"No, I don't ever have to have known anything," Barnett said. "I hurt him. Once, half a lifetime ago, I hurt him. That's all it would take. I suppose he thought at first he wouldn't have to get even with me. He thought life would take care of that for him. After all, in nineteen forty-one, what was a *nigger boy* to be worth revenge?" There was infinite bitterness in his voice. "But then—"

He looked up. "He's been gone. He's got to have been gone. He just got back in town six or eight months ago. Because that's when it started, the letters and the phone calls, and it would have started sooner if he'd been here. Because I've been—God knows I've been prominent enough, the last twenty years. And controversial enough. I mean, I'm no Julian Bond, but they know I'm here, the white racists know I'm here. The black racists say I don't do enough, but the white racists—and he is that. He is that. He doesn't just hate me as a person. He's—I wish I had saved those letters. I wish I hadn't thrown them away. Then I could make you see what I mean. But they were too filthy to keep. And they upset Cynthia. I tried to keep her from seeing them."

"You never told me any of that," Smoky said.

"Why should I? It was just filth, just hate words."

"No," Smoky said, "not just filth and hate words. Evidence. A person's personality gets into letters, and furthermore, his fingerprints get onto them. That's the kind of thing that might help us find him."

"Then at least you concede there is a him to find."

"I don't know that for a fact," Simons told him. "Since you're demanding frankness, no, I still don't know that. But I am at the moment proceeding on the assumption that there is someone to find."

"And," Smoky said, "I am proceeding on the assumption the same person killed Libby Bonner and attacked your wife."

"But—God—we've got too much to work on right now," Simons said wearily. He'd been working for nearly two months on his one solid—he thought—lead on Rosemary and it hadn't panned out. And he knew that Smoky (who had been pulled off Rosemary because Captain Cardew said he was too emotionally involved to work on it) had been just as tirelessly following up dead ends on Mary Thomas.

Meanwhile the usual work of the bureau—the thefts, the burglaries, the not-too-frequent robberies and muggings, the salesmen rolled by the whores, and the stolen cars and the stolen CB radios—went on at their usual rate, with the other detectives working on them. The lieutenants and the captains worked on the things that promised to be long-range.

At first glance this one was more urgent because this person's victim was still alive and he would possibly (probably?) try again. But was it really that much more urgent than Rosemary? Smoky and Steve had finally put their heads together and agreed they likely would have the same person on both Rosemary and Mary Thomas, which meant he could hit again at any time. If he hadn't already. Mary Thomas had been dead awhile before they found her.

They exchanged tired glances. "We don't need to ask you anything else right now," Simons told him. "You got anymore to ask us?"

"Not really." He stood up. "I'll be at home awhile. I need to get some rest."

"If you can think of anything else at all, you let us know," Smoky said. "Even if it seems totally insignificant to you."

The man who liked to kill women was aware the police had been called in on his blackmail attempts. He'd expected they would be. It didn't bother him. He knew enough about how police work that he didn't figure they'd find him. And if they did they couldn't prove anything, not unless they knew exactly where to look.

He'd never killed a man. He didn't want to kill this man. It was more interesting to watch him squirm, like a box of fishing worms left open in the sun. He hadn't killed the woman—that man's woman—because this one time it had been more interesting not to. This was like playing a game. He'd started it out months ago just for revenge, but now it was like a puzzle just for its own sake, keep the man guessing what he was going to do.

That first barrage of letters and phone calls had been preliminaries, feeling his way, finding out how the man reacted to stress and needling. Then he'd begun to plan, a little along, watching the reaction to each step before he planned the next one.

At the moment he didn't know himself what he was going to do next. He'd made a dumb move. He'd gone up to the hospital and found the woman was in a room that had a sign on the door, "Immediate Family Only." He wasn't going to hurt her, just leave some kind of note or something, but when he stuck his head in, there was a woman sitting on a chair in the corner. She wasn't a nurse and quite obviously she wasn't family. She was a rather small woman, with wispy blond hair and a dangly necklace, but she looked at him, looked at him hard. He hadn't known Farmer's Mound had policewomen, but there was something in the set of her eyes—and he had to think of something to say in a hurry and it was on top of his mind, he said, "Is this Libby Bonner's room?" and she'd said, "No, it isn't," and he'd left.

Thinking back on it now made him sweat. He didn't know why in the *hell* he'd said—but it was on top of his mind, that name, and maybe she wouldn't remember. (She would remember, though, because cops remember. And she was a cop because only cops look at people like that,

120

other people look and then look away because it isn't polite to stare. Only cops stare.)

He wondered if anybody was back at that house yet. He guessed the man would go out there eventually—but—damn! The man would have to rest, but so would he. He'd hardly had any sleep at all in two days. Maybe he'd think of an idea while he was asleep. Sometimes that happened.

"Look," Smoky said to George Revills, quite politely, "you've been real cooperative with us, and we appreciate it. It makes it a lot easier all around. But you lied to us about one thing, and it shows because in everything else you haven't lied. So we'd really like to know why."

"I don't remember lying about anything," Revills said. And he was an old hand, he wasn't going to be taken in by the good-cop bad-cop role-playing, but he was damn scared of something.

"Yes, you did," Simons said from the other side of him. "You lied when you said you didn't know Libby Bonner. And we don't know why, because we know you didn't kill her and we figure from what you say that you hadn't gone into the abortion business until after she was killed. So we really don't understand why you lied about knowing her."

Revills shook his head. "Look, I didn't kill her and I don't know who did, so just let it alone, would you?"

He had slipped a lot from the suaveness he'd shown the night before. They were seeing a little, now, of the raw edges of the old George Revills, the one-night-stand musician whose parties all turned into brawls. "What instrument do you play?" Smoky asked conversationally.

"Clarinet. What's that got to do with—anyway, I play a lot of instruments, but I guess you mean what did I play professionally. And it was a clarinet."

"Okay. I was just curious. Look, if you didn't kill Libby and you don't know who did, why won't you tell us what you *do* know?"

"What the hell's about Libby?" the man shouted.

"Look, she's dead and buried, she's been dead over forty *years* for God's sake, what the hell difference—"

"I don't remember telling you when she was killed," Smoky said softly.

"All right, God damn it, yes, I know when she was—but I just don't understand why you need to know. It doesn't matter now."

"But it does," Smoky said. "Let me put it this way. I accept your reasons for abortion. That doesn't mean I agree with you. Happens I don't. But I see your line of reasoning and I accept it as valid for you. With me so far?"

"I hear you," Revills said cautiously.

"Well," Smoky went on, sitting on the edge of the desk and moving a little closer to Revills, "if I accept your line of reasoning as valid, then I'm assuming you don't like for women to get hurt. Am I still right?"

"Yeah," Revills said doubtfully, a wary look on his face.

"Well, I'm telling you, whoever killed Libby Bonner, and yes, I know how long ago that was, but all the same he's loose now and he's here now and he's still attacking women. If you'll tell us what you know it might help us to stop him."

"Look, damn it," Revills burst out, the look on his face now verging on panic, "I admit, I did know her, but what I know about her, it didn't have anything at all to do with—"

"You tell us and let us decide that," Smoky said.

"All right, all right, all *right!* Just—what the hell, I don't care if you know, just so long as it doesn't—can I have some coffee?"

"Yeah, sure," Smoky said, but made no move to go for any.

"But not till after I tell you, right?"

"I didn't say that," Smoky answered. He went over to the coffeepot, poured a cup, and came back. "Now you want to tell us about it?"

122

"No, I don't. But—all right. I—damn it, you know part of what I was doing, but not all. You never will know all of it because there's no way—but in forty-one I was trying to set me up a string."

A string of call girls. He'd been a pimp. They should have guessed, they'd already traced his connection to several old-time whores, and eventually one of them would have thought of it. But not yet.

"So I was trying to get her—hell, she already was one, but she didn't know how to do business, she was selling herself too cheap. She was a pretty woman and she knew how to—and I treated them right, I never did go in for rough stuff, it just isn't necessary. You treat a girl decent, she'll do you a better job and besides that she's happier about it. But I went over to her house that afternoon. She was expecting me at five o'clock, I had her a date set up for a century and damn, in those days that was money, you know? But then I found her. God. Do you know what she looked like? Do you?"

"We know," Smoky said.

"So I—I got out of there and I called the police and didn't give my name and I told them so they'd find her body before she got to—got to stinking."

That was in the report. Dispatcher was notified by an anonymous telephone call, voice sounded like a young white male.

"Anything else you can tell us?"

"I didn't kill her!"

"We know you didn't kill her," Smoky said. "We didn't ask if you did."

"You do know?" Revills asked doubtfully. "I thought you were just saying that to get me started talking."

"We have an eyewitness to the killing," Smoky told him. "That's what the lineup was about. He told us it wasn't you. But he doesn't have much of anything else about who it could have been except a vague description. Can you tell us anything else?"

"She said—she told me one time," Revills said, sounding a little calmer now, "that if anyone ever took her off—that was her phrase, 'takes me off'—that if anyone ever took her off, to look for her ex-husband. She said he was crazy—crazy jealous and crazy mean. But she said he always carried a gun. And she damn sure wasn't killed with no gun."

"No, she wasn't," Smoky agreed. "Do you know who her ex-husband was?"

"No, I don't. I just met her early in forty-one and she'd been divorced sometime about nineteen forty. One thing—she told me she better not ever get in trouble because her husband was the one who took care of girls in trouble, and he used to talk about getting a knife and just turning it—she didn't finish talking about that."

Oh my God, Smoky thought. But all he said was, "Anything else?"

"No."

"Okay. Look, I'll tell the judge you've cooperated with us. That make you feel any better?"

"What am I going to wind up charged with?"

"We already told you that," Captain Simons said.

"Tell me again."

"Criminal abortion and practicing medicine without a license."

"Look," Revills said, with fear evident in his eyes again. "I'll plead guilty, only don't let the papers make a big deal of it, so it sounds like I'm in active business again, and don't let them know anything about the string. Can you do that? Because if you can I'll see what I can maybe find out about Libby Bonner, from some sources you might not know about. But—"

Smoky eyed him dispassionately. "I believe," he said, "that you got tired of working for the big boys, and went to trying to poach in their territory. Didn't you?"

Revills was silent for a moment. Then he said slowly, "You could put it that way."

"Do they know you're here?"

124

"They suggested I retire. For my health. Yes, they probably know I'm here. They don't care, as long as I stay retired."

"We'll try to keep it quiet for you," Simons told him, "on condition."

"On condition of what? Because I've told you all I know about Libby. Honest to God I have."

"On condition," Simons said, "that you retire and stay retired. For," he added blandly, "your health."

"I think that's extortion," Revills said slowly. But the corners of his mouth were twitching, and then he gave up and grinned. "I think I can agree to that."

"Well, we'll send you back to jail now," Simons told him. "I'll see to it you get a chance to call your lawyer."

"I don't want to call my lawyer," Revills said. "My lawyer—well, my lawyer—"

"Was one of the big boys," Smoky supplied.

"You know too damn much," Revills said. "Just call the district attorney. I don't need a lawyer to plead guilty."

"All right," Simons said, and escorted him back to the jail. He returned shaking his head. "He asked me four times on the way up there when he could cop a plea. He obviously figures to get probation."

"Would you care to place any bets he won't?" Smoky answered.

"I'm not a betting man. But if I was I'd be betting he will." Simons looked up at the big wall clock. "Let's go get a hot dog."

The day was sweltering hot. They stayed mostly in the shade of the store awnings, envying the beat cop's open-necked white shirt and knowing the beat cop envied their air-conditioned car.

The cafe was dimly lit and cool, a gratefully welcomed relief after the glare of the sidewalk. It was an old building, and even though air conditioning was working the old ceiling fans were also turning. Quite possibly the first

Farmer's Mound policemen, their names nearly forgotten now, had come here to eat; certainly those men, now no more than names on reports, who had originally investigated Libby Bonner's murder had eaten here.

Nineteen forty-one. It is only yesterday on the calendar; Pearl Harbor is not forgotten. But Libby Bonner had died before Pearl Harbor, and the young men who fought that war have adult grandchildren now. Neither Steve Simons nor Smoky O'Donnell could remember Pearl Harbor. And rookies are not made detectives. The men who worked that murder were born in the nineteenth century.

Nineteen forty-one is not so long ago. Until you try to find out what happened then.

"Are you thinking what I'm thinking?" Simons asked.

"Yeah," Smoky said.

"The same man," Simons said. "The same damn man. And somehow—" He looked around; there were too many ears for him to name names. "Somehow Davey must have known something or X was afraid he did. But why the hell haven't we realized X had to know Davey? I just thought of it."

"We know he saw him," Smoky began, and stopped. "Of course, I see what you mean."

"But he had to know who he was. There's a hundred boys like Davey on the street, no way to pick him out over any of the others. But X knew him not just as any twelve-year-old. X knew him by name."

"So? That doesn't necessarily mean he really knew him. He could have just known where he worked."

"Uh-uh," Simons said. "That won't work, Smoke. Because he said that first note he got, the very next day, was stuck in his mother's mailbox."

"Well, how can we—I don't know what we can do about finding out who would have—anyhow, Steve, that doesn't make sense."

"Why doesn't it?"

"Who is it that would recognize him but he wouldn't

126

recognize? Kids are more observant than adults. Most kids recognize a lot of people who don't recognize them. But this is somebody who recognized Davey and Davey didn't recognize him. Now, who the hell—"

"Brainstorm. Neighborhood? No, he lived in an all-black neighborhood. School? Maybe a teacher in another classroom?"

"Won't work. Nineteen forty-one. Segregated schools, remember?"

"Oh, yeah." Simons shook his head. "Autumn Hill. Damn it, he delivered groceries in Autumn Hill. Maybe —Autumn Hill was mixed. It was about the only mixed neighborhood there was then."

"God, if we just knew who lived there. Look, is there any way in the world we can trace down who her ex-husband was?"

They applied themselves to hot dogs and coffee in glum silence. Then they went back to the office, and Smoky went to the records section. Jeff Kirk was at his desk eating a tunafish sandwich and reading a paperback. "Jeff," Smoky said, in his most persuasive voice.

"I'm eating," Kirk said instantly, with his mouth full. "Look it up yourself, whatever it is."

Bonner. She was twenty-four when she died. Presumably he was the same age or older. DOB in 1917 or earlier.

But her husband might not ever have been arrested. And if he had it might have been for something minor, like traffic or drunk, that would later have been culled out if the record had stayed inactive so many years.

Bonner, Andrew. B/M. Bonner, Bobbie Jo. W/F DOB 3-11-53. Bonner, Carolyn. Bonner, Elizabeth. W/F 6-19-17. AKA Libby. "Dec." someone had scrawled across it. So she had a little record, more than traffic or disorderly, or it would have been thrown away. Normally, now, a victim's record would routinely go in the case jacket. So he hadn't thought—he pulled the card out, to check later, and went on looking.

Bonner, Frederick. W/M 2-19-15. A possible—No. Shit. Check the descriptions. 5'4''. Unless that was a typographical error, that couldn't be Barnett's very tall man, and with a weight of 105 it wasn't a typographical error.

Bonner, Robert Lee. B/M. Bonner, Samuel. B/M. Bonner, Thomas Frederick. W/M 5-4-46. Bonner, William B/M.

And that was all the Bonners.

Smoky became aware of a raging headache. He closed the file drawer and pulled out the record on Elizabeth Bonner. Drunk. Drunk and fighting. CCW—carrying a concealed weapon. Drunk. Cussed other woman at Rose's Bar, drunk, resisted arrest. No busts for prostitution. And the whole record covered a bare eight months.

A fire in the courthouse in 1950 had destroyed old vital statistics. It would be impossible to find divorce records.

He went and pulled out her mug shot. Even in the old black and white print she was pretty, a woman you'd notice in a crowd. But that said nothing now.

He went back in the detective bureau and said, "I have an idea. But it would be one hell of a lot of work."

"So what isn't?" The captain's desk was an untidy heap of case jackets—Libby Bonner, Rosemary Waters, Mary Thomas, Cynthia Barnett—and he was looking very unhappy.

"Well, if the library would let us bring that nineteen forty-one directory over here, and if we got last year's city directory and this year's city directory, we could maybe find out who was living around Autumn Hill in nineteen forty-one and wasn't in town last year and is this year."

"Damnation," Simons answered. "You do think of the most complicated—but it just might work."

They went to the library.

The library regretted it could not let its only copy of the 1941 city directory be taken out of the library. Smoky was persuasive. The library regretted—Simons also was persuasive.

Well, if they'd be very careful with it—

The task was unreal. Autumn Hill doesn't seem that big, when you're driving through it in a marked car or answering a call to a shooting. A few blocks, shot houses and duplexes and ratty stucco apartments and old mill houses. Not much. You get a call and you go to it. But on paper. On paper. Autumn Hill Road cuts through at an angle. Six blocks of Antuna Street. Six blocks of Chase Road. Six blocks of Hill Street. Six blocks of Home Street. All crossing four blocks of Spring Avenue and four blocks of Elsie Avenue and four blocks of Duell Road and four blocks of Chance Street. With Dellwood Court cutting across Autumn Hill Road and Duell Road at an odd little angle.

A lot of blocks. A lot of houses.

And he might never have gotten into the directory at all. Unless a person is living at the place at the time the interviewer comes by, the name won't get in the book. A drifter might move four or five times in a year.

A lot of names. A lot of people.

No Bonners. Not even Libby.

When Captain Cardew came in at three-thirty, the two had pushed their desks together and both desks were piled with paper. Even with the air conditioning on it was 82 degrees in the room and they were both sweating. He looked at them. "Think you're onto something?"

"If you want to be honest," Simons told him, "no, we don't. We're grasping at straws."

He watched them a minute longer. "I want both of you to listen to me," he said softly. And he and Simons were both captains, but he was ten years older and had fourteen years more experience than Simons, and the chief had made it very plain to all concerned who was chief of detectives. "You've both been working nights and days off for months, and you're both so tired you can't think straight. I'm giving you a direct order. I want both of you out of here no later than four-thirty and I don't want either of you back here before seven-thirty tomorrow morning.

And no running around just checking on this and that on your own time. I want you both to get some rest. Do I make myself clear?"

They assured him, in somewhat less than cheerful tones, that he had made himself clear. Then they both went back to work. "Hey," Simons said, "how about the postman?"

Smoky looked up, eyes startled. "You could be—"

They called the post office. The postmaster said he'd check, but he didn't think he could possibly find—and he hoped they didn't need it immediately because he couldn't possibly—

They went back to the city directory.

IX

"ALL EIGHT TO four units not ten-six, signal twenty-five," the radio said cheerfully. Out in the hall, the four-to-twelve shift was leaving muster, noisily signing for radios and cars and preparing to hit the street. In the parking lot, sirens whined briefly as oncoming men checked out their cars.

Tommy Inman wandered into the detective bureau, his six-foot-two bulk looking even bigger indoors than out. "Smoky? Steve?" he said diffidently. "Can you guys go over to the county clerk's office with me right now?"

They wanted to work till four-thirty, but Simons answered, "Yeah, sure."

"Because Melissa's already up there," Tommy explained.

The county clerk's office in Texas keeps track of birth certificates, death certificates, and everything in between. Besides issuing marriage licenses, it also is empowered to perform marriages. And that, the two surmised as they crossed the street to the courthouse, was why they had been requested to go there.

Melissa, in a pink sundress with her long blond hair straight down her back, was almost inaudible; Tommy seemed almost nonchalant to anybody not watching his eyes. Afterward Tommy said, "Where's the car?" Melissa pointed vaguely toward the city parking lot and handed the key, which was hanging from a large pink puff, to Tommy.

Outside the building, Steve said, "Any other couple, I'd figure they were going to a motel. Those two, I figure they're going home. So I don't want to. Would Audra mind if I invaded you for a while?"

"No, if you don't mind the confusion. You know with the baby she hasn't got much time for the house."

At eight-thirty Simons quietly let himself in the front door, figuring to slip on up to his room. But Tommy was sitting on the couch in faded blue jeans, with his feet on the coffee table again, and Melissa was curled on the couch with her head on his lap. Tommy looked up, put a finger to his lips, pointed to Melissa's head, and made a gesture that said "Sleep." Steve nodded, wondering what they were doing up anyway.

He closed the door quietly, but not quietly enough. Melissa half sat up. "Hi," she said drowsily, sounding not quite awake.

"Hi," he answered.

"I'm sleepy," she said. "What di' we get up for?"

"Cause you wanted a sandwich," Tommy reminded her.

"Did I? Yeah, I did want a sandwich. Now I want to go back to bed." She stumbled for the stairs.

"Okay, okay," Tommy said, following her. "I'll take a shower and be there in a minute."

"I'll take a shower too."

"You'll get your hair wet."

" 'S already wet." And she still was not awake. "Got all sweaty."

"Then you can wash it in the morning. Look out, Lissa, don't trip on the stairs."

Steve Simons could not remember the last time he had seen Melissa relaxed. For months, it seemed, she had been tensely nervous over one thing or another. But suddenly he didn't want to spend this night in the house. "Tommy," he said quietly, "I'll be back later."

" 'Kay."

Melissa didn't notice him leave; he wasn't quite sure she'd ever noticed him arrive.

For want of anything better to do, he decided to go to Sambo's and get a cup of coffee. All the booths were full, but the "Please seat yourself" sign still had not been replaced by the one that read "Please Wait to be Seated." There was one woman about his age sitting alone at a table for two. He walked toward her, carefully threading his way through the crowd. "Do you mind if I join you?" he asked politely, and in the time it took him to say the sentence he recognized her. "Florence?"

He shouldn't be that surprised; it was the only decent place in town to get a cup of coffee at this time of night, but it had been so long—

"Certainly, I—" She started to answer before looking at him, then she hesitated. "Steve? Oh, for goodness' sake! I haven't seen you since—do sit down! Of course it had to be you, who else ever had hair that color? I'd heard you were in the police department, but I guess I must have misunderstood, because—"

He laughed involuntarily. "You still talk as fast as ever. Yes, I'm a police captain, and what have you been doing for the last twenty-five years?"

"I'm a free-lance photographer, and don't say it's a funny job, because everybody says that and I—"

"Why not? You always used to take a lot of pictures. But why did you think you had misunderstood about my job?"

"Well—" Abruptly her animation subsided, and she looked down at her coffee cup. "Well, I never saw you, and I thought I saw just about everybody on the police department when my husband was killed."

"Killed?" He hadn't seen Florence Pietra since high school. He'd assumed she married but didn't know to whom, and certainly didn't know what she was talking about now.

133

"Yes, Jack Inman. I thought—"

"Lord, I didn't know. I was in traffic when that happened." It was a particularly brutal holdup and murder four years back, and Steve suspected it had been the shock of it that had precipitated Tommy into his brief fling with drugs and motorcycle gangs. "I never realized that was your husband. But then, my gosh, you're Tommy's mother!"

"Yes. I've been out of town, you know. I just got back tonight—" She was rather obviously changing the subject—"thinking I was back home in Texas where everything would be nice and quiet, and look at this place!"

"I'm afraid you've walked in on the aftermath of a baseball game," he explained. "A lot of the teams and their families come over here after the games. But when did you get back to town? Tommy wasn't expecting you for another month. Damn, I wish we'd known you were back."

"Well, you do seem to know Tommy!" she said. "I got in all of half an hour ago and thought I'd eat here before I started thinking about unpacking. There's not anything wrong, is there?"

"No. But your son and my daughter were married at four-thirty this afternoon."

"Married!" She looked startled, as he guessed she had a right to do. "Well, I'll admit I don't stay in touch as well as I should, but it does seem they could have waited another month."

"There was a little problem," he said, wondering how to put it gracefully. "Tommy has—well, the kids were trying to play straight, I'm sure of that, but—things got a little out of control once and once is all it takes. You and I, lady, are going to be grandparents in about seven months."

"Oh," she said. "Do you have a picture of her with you?"

He took it out of his billfold and slid it over. As she studied it, he looked at her. He hadn't seen her in twenty-odd years, as hard as that was to believe with them both living in the same small town, but they didn't live in the same neighborhood, or go to the same church, or shop at the same stores, or join the same clubs. There'd just been no reason.

She hadn't really changed that much, and she didn't look like somebody likely to be the mother of a very large twenty-three-year-old cop. At least—well—he knew she was forty-two (the six months older than him that she was had once been the grounds for considerable teasing) but she was a rather small woman. She had curly salt-and-pepper hair, very blue eyes, and a squared-off jaw. Her hands were small and square-looking with no rings at all.

No jewelry of any kind, in fact.

That, he guessed, was a habit. He remembered her in high school on the yearbook staff, doing all the darkroom work for the numerous candid photographs that went into the book. She didn't wear jewelry then, either. She said the chemicals didn't help it much, and it was too hard to remember to take it off.

She handed the picture back. "She's very pretty. I'd been awfully worried about who he might wind up with while he was running around with those awful people over in Dallas. But what are you doing out by yourself?"

"Didn't want to go home," he explained. "The kids went over there. And I just wanted to give them some privacy."

"I see. Well, in that case, why don't you come over to my house and let me give you a drink? That might give our—offspring—time to settle down."

"I hate to impose," he said. "You've been gone so long."

"For months and two days exactly. But I had somebody go in and dust everything off for me day before yesterday,

135

when I decided to go home. And if you don't come over I'll feel compelled to start unpacking tonight and that's a task I loathe."

"In that case," he said and laughed, "I'll follow you over. No, I've got the coffee."

Tommy hadn't liked this house. In one way, hadn't liked this woman. But that was because things had gone wrong and maybe, now, things were going right. There was a big round hassock in front of the couch. "I think I'd better get one of those things," Steve said.

"Why?"

"So Tommy will keep his feet off the coffee table."

"Is he still doing that? That's why I got it, his dad had the same habit. Bourbon all right?"

"Yes. Just a little water."

And she was, he thought, a damn pretty woman still, in an unusual way. And they had been a lot more than friends once, a long time ago. His lips began to curve into a reminiscent smile, and he looked away from her at his glass.

"What are you grinning about?"

"Just wondering," he said, "if you still have a mole where you used to have a mole." If he had any questions in his mind as to whether she could still blush, they were instantly answered.

It was, in all, a pleasant evening. It might not have been what Cardew meant by resting. But it certainly got his mind off his work.

"What are you doing up so early?"

"I thought I'd make coffee," Tommy said. "There's no use Melissa having to get up this early on Saturday, but I've got to go to work."

"So do I, but never mind the coffee. I went to Sambo's last night and came across an old school friend of mine, and I promised her I'd meet her there for breakfast and bring you along. If you can haul your bride out of bed and make her put some clothes on, she can come too."

"Why?"

"Well, because the lady is your mother."

"Huh?" He turned. "When did she get back to town?"

"Last night."

"Okay," Tommy said, and went up the stairs. A moment later the sound of Melissa being sick was more than usually audible. Tommy came back downstairs. "She says she's not getting up this morning. She says it's Saturday and she doesn't have to go to school and her stomach hurts and she hates breakfast."

"Sounds like a truly glorious honeymoon. You have to go to work and she's morning sick."

"Oh well," Tommy said. "As long as I don't have to go on four to twelve. Because she's fine at night." He picked up his gunbelt from where he'd dropped it on the table. "I didn't know you knew my mother."

"I didn't either, because her name wasn't Inman when I knew her," Steve said. "But we went steady, as the phrase was in those days, for two years. I'm going to enjoy getting reacquainted with her."

"Good grief," Tommy said.

In the car he said, thoughtfully, "I didn't mean to sound rude awhile ago. I just can't see you being apeshit over my mother."

"Why not? You seem to be a little apeshit, and that's an idiotic phrase by the way, over my daughter."

"Yeah, but that's different. Mom's so damn clingy."

"Yeah. She's so damn clingy that she realized she was making you uncomfortable. So she went a thousand miles away to take photographs, leaving you working undercover and her terrified you'd get hurt. She loves you, Tommy."

"Yeah, I know."

In Sambo's he dutifully hugged her, looked embarrassed as she exclaimed over his haircut, uniform, and weight, and then, obviously relieved that was over, paid attention to coffee. Almost through with his first cup, he glanced out the window and stiffened. "Steve," he said, "out the window. Real casual, but look."

"It's Eddie Reno. So?"

"We've—me and Smoky—we've got a warrant on him for heroin. And he knows who killed Mary Thomas. He didn't. But he knows who did."

"Okay. For now, stay put. Let him get away from the car. Does he carry a gun?"

"I've never known him to, except that time when he got mine, but then he gave it to Buck and Buck gave it back to me."

"Damn it, if we had a radio—"

"He'll be coming inside," Tommy said. "That's one good thing, I think everybody in town comes here. He's never seen me with short hair. He might not recognize me at once, but I'm so damn *big*—"

"He doesn't know me."

"Shit he doesn't know you. He told me one time he knows every plainclothesman in town from the back as well as from the front. Look away from him." Tommy put his hand up, to hide his face from the sidewalk. "He can't miss the uniform, but if he doesn't know it's me he might not know a uniform man would be looking for him. Mama. Watch him. What's he doing?"

"The man with the long sandy hair, that got out of the green car?"

"Yeah, him. What's he doing?"

"He's not paying you any attention. He's just walking toward the door."

Then he was seated at the counter, in a position that had him and Tommy at right angles facing away from each other, and he might know all the plainclothesmen but he hadn't spotted Simons yet. He wasn't really paying any attention when they both got up and walked toward him, but then he noticed and where the gun in his hand came from neither of them even knew, but he grabbed a waitress with

138

the other hand and there it was, that fast, a hostage situation.

What every cop dreads most. Because the cops accept the risks but have no right to inflict them on the civilian.

They should have tried to take him outside, but it was too late to decide that now.

They both froze, hands well away from their guns, and now, facing him, they could see what they hadn't earlier. He was hopped up on something, bad. And he was scared. "You ain't gonna take me in!" he shouted. "You told! You told! You ain't gonna—you want to hurt me—"

"Told what?" Simons asked, in utter bewilderment.

But Eddie was watching Tommy. "You wanta—you ain't gonna—"

"Nobody wants to hurt you, Eddie," Tommy said, very quietly, not moving, his eyes intent on the wavering gun barrel. "Nobody wants to hurt you. Me and Buck made a deal, remember? It's just, there's a warrant on you for drugs. It's not much, you've had a drug bust before."

"No! You tryin' to trick me, you want to—you told!"

"No, I didn't tell. Are you scared of me?"

Eddie glanced around, desperately. "Hey! You get away from that phone, you trying to call—don't you try—"

Hastily, the assistant manager backed away from the phone.

It was a miracle nobody had panicked and started screaming; the place was incredibly silent. "You ain't scared of me, Eddie, are you?" Tommy asked. "Because I'm still Tommy. I'm still the same dude I always was."

"No! I ain't scared—I ain't scared of Tommy Inman. But—"

"Okay, listen. There's a dope warrant out. We want to arrest you for that warrant, and that's all."

"Then why'd you go to my mama's house the next day? She tole me that you wanna—"

"No. I don't want to hurt you. I really don't, Eddie, I

139

don't want to hurt you. We went over there because we wanted to ask you who wanted you to move the chifforobe, and that's the only reason."

"No! You told them other cops. You wanna get me in jail and hit me. You—"

"I'll tell you what, Eddie. There's a whole room full of people in here. Why don't I do this? I'll tell them all —right now—what you're scared of. Then I couldn't possibly hurt you, could I? Because if I did all of them would know it was me done it, and they'd tell the FBI and the FBI would come get me. That sound like a deal?"

"That's okay," Eddie said.

"If I do that then will you give me the gun?"

Eddie gulped. "Yeah. But remember, you promised me am—amnes—you promised I don't go to jail for it."

"Okay. I promised about that, but you know you still got to go to jail for other stuff. Listen, everybody, okay?" (As if there was a person in the place who wasn't listening already.) "This guy here, his name is Eddie Reno. And he's scared, because a few months ago I was working undercover and Eddie and some of his friends found out about it. So they took my gun away from me and beat me up and Eddie wanted to kill me, but we made a deal that if they wouldn't kill me I wouldn't try to do anything about them beating me up. But we do have a drug case on Eddie, and he's scared I'm going to get him in jail and then try to get even for what he did then. But I'm not and you all heard me say it. Okay, Eddie. Give me the gun now."

"You ain't gonna—?" The gun barrel wavered even more, and Simons watched it. If it had been a revolver he might, just might, have taken the chance and grabbed for it, but it was a big Army Colt .45 automatic and Eddie's finger was on the trigger.

"No," Tommy said, watching the gun barrel waver fourteen inches from his abdomen, "nobody's going to hurt you. Can I have the gun now, Eddie?"

And Eddie laid the gun on the counter, turned the girl

loose, and very docilely turned around and put his hands behind his back to be handcuffed. "Okay," Tommy said, "Captain Simons is going to call for a police car to take you in. You want you and me to go out and lock up your car, so's nobody steals anything out of it?"

"My car?" Eddie looked stricken. "I guess I got to tell you about that, don't I?"

"You don't have to tell me anything. You have the right—"(I'm really doing it, he thought. This is what I told Smoky I'd do and I'm really doing it. And I honestly don't *want* to get even for him stomping me.)

"Yeah, I understand all that," Eddie said. "But if I leave it in the car somebody'll steal it so I better tell you."

"What, then?"

"The money. Out of that safe."

"Safe?" Tommy repeated, wondering what he was talking about.

"That safe at the loan company. It was a lot of money."

"Trinity Finance?" Captain Simons asked.

"Yeah. Cause my mama borrowed the money from them to get another refrigerator when her old one conked out. And I went down there with her one day about five o'clock to make a payment and I seed where they kept the money. So I went back the other night and got it."

"I see," the captain said. "Was it by any chance you who went into Texas Loan?"

"No, that was Skeet. You know Skeet?"

"Yeah, I know Skeet. Okay. You want to show Tommy where the money is, while I call for a uniform car?"

"Yeah, I guess."

And there it was, ten green plastic bank bags stuffed into a brown paper grocery sack, in the right front floorboard of the old green Pontiac. "What are you gonna do with it?" Eddie asked.

"Leave it right there, for now. I guess we'll give it back to the finance company as soon as we get pictures of it."

Simons, who had joined them, said, "We got a car on

the way, and another one going out to pick up Skeet. Tommy, after breakfast you can drive this car in."

"Here's the keys," Eddie said cheerfully. "And you wanta watch out for them brakes. You understand," he said earnestly, "I just didn't want nobody to steal it. Because one time I went into a bar and got some stuff and hid it, and when I went back to get it somebody had stoled it. So I didn't want—"

"I promise, Eddie, we won't let nobody steal it."

"Say, Tommy, how in the hell do you get to be a cop?" Eddie asked earnestly. " 'Cause I think—"

Tommy raised stricken eyes to his father-in-law, who hastily looked away and drew his hand over his mouth.

"He didn't want anybody to steal it?" Smoky repeated with raised eyebrows.

"Well, you remember that thing at the Black Cat," Jerry reminded him. "I got his prints off the money box from the pinball machine and he 'fessed up to the burglary and went out to show us where he left the stuff, and it was gone. And we never did find out who ripped him off."

"So he didn't—oh, brother," Smoky said.

"And then he wanted to be a *cop*!" Simons yelped, giving way to the laughter he'd had to suppress earlier.

Smoky looked at the closed door to the interview room. "Let me look back over this case jacket on Thomas. Then I'll go in and talk with him."

"Captain?" Linn put her head in at the office door. "Something happened yesterday, and I didn't think much about it then, but I got to thinking you might ought to know about it."

"Yeah?"

She came on in and sat down. "Well, it wasn't much. But a guy got in the room by mistake, said he was looking for somebody else, and I told him that wasn't her room and he left."

142

"So why's that important?"

"Because I got curious about it and checked. And there's nobody by that name in the hospital or even in their files at all. It was Bonner. Libby Bonner."

"Oh, my God," Smoky said.

"What—is that important?" She looked at him. "Did I miss something?"

"You had him. That was—what did he look like?"

"White male, about—oh, I guess sixty-five or so. He certainly didn't look dangerous. Quite tall, I'd guess maybe six-five, slender build, grey hair. I didn't notice his eyes. Rather untidy looking. He was clean shaven but smelled like he maybe needed a bath."

"Okay," Smoky said, "go look through the mug books and see if you can find him."

She hesitated. "I'm supposed to relieve Kay at the hospital."

"Kay's going to have to wait. Go check the mug books," Simons told her.

Smoky went back into the interview room. "Hello, Eddie."

"Hey," Eddie said nervously.

"That wasn't very good manners, pulling a gun on Tommy," Smoky said conversationally. "Second time you've done it, too."

"Yeah, but the other time it wasn't my gun."

"And this time it was. You're just breaking all kind of laws, Eddie. Let's see, carrying a firearm, carrying a concealed weapon, possessing a weapon in the commission of a crime—you used to have better sense than that. That's a hell of a big gun, too. Where'd you get it?"

"I stoled it off a dead nigger."

"You done no such thing," Smoky said. "Where'd you get the gun?"

"I stoled it off a drunk in a bar. He was passed out and I didn't figure he needed it noway."

143

"Where was the bar?"

"In Galveston. And don't ask me where in Galveston or what the guy looked like 'cause I don't remember. I was drunk too."

"Then I guess we'll run it on NCIC and find out who it belongs to," Smoky said. "Now let's talk about the chifforobe."

"What chifforobe? I don't know nothing about no chifforobe."

"That chifforobe you wanted Tommy and Buck to help you move last month. That chifforobe that dude was going to give you so much bread to move. That chifforobe."

His jaw twitched sideways. "I don't know nothing about no chifforobe. Somebody's pulling your leg."

Smoky looked at him. He was a dirty little man, the chin-length sandy hair streaked with grease. His hands were grimy and it was impossible to determine what color his now sort-of-beige shirt had started out to be. His eyes were pale blue. And he was scared. Very damn scared. Smoky kept on looking at him.

"I told you I don't know nothing about no chifforobe!" he shouted.

"Yes, you do," Smoky said evenly.

"Look, I don't—I don't know nothing about no killing."

"Okay. I didn't ask you about the killing. I just asked about the chifforobe."

"I never went over there till me and Tommy and Buck all together did, except just to look in the window, and then when I got inside—that guy, he lied to me!"

"All right. What guy?"

"I don't know what guy."

"He was gonna give you so much bread that you could spare a century for Tommy and Buck, but you don't know who he was?" Smoky started tearing open a package of cigarettes.

"Hey, look, gimme one of those, would you?"

"Okay," Smoky said, and lit it for him. "Now tell me about the guy."

"I don't know him! I met him in a bar. It was—there was a bunch of dudes talking and he said he'd give a lot of money to have just a little job done and I ast him what little job and he said if I was interested meet him outside and I did and he tole me—and I tole Tommy all I know and I don't know no more and I don't know who he was, he give me the key to the place and he said after the job was done I could meet him back at the bar and he'd give me the money and I don't know what guy."

"What's he look like?"

"I can't—just a guy, I know him if I see him. An ol' dude."

A curious feeling was beginning at the back of Smoky's neck; suddenly this was fitting right in with what George Revills had said. An old dude. "How tall was he?"

"I don't know. I never measured him for God's sake. He was a lot taller than me."

"Does he have any kind of scar?" Smoky asked.

"I never noticed no scar," Eddie said. "But look, I just talked to him a little while, at the bar."

"What bar?"

"The—the—" He suddenly looked frantic. "Look, I don't want you to think—I don't go there regular, it was just, I had me a powerful thirst an' I just stopped in there just for a beer, you know, an'—"

"Okay. I understand. You don't go there regular. What bar are we talking about?"

"The—the Red Herring," Eddie got out, looking very embarrassed.

The Red Herring. The local gay bar. Now that was something to think about. "Okay, Eddie," Smoky said absently, "I know you ain't no queer, if that's what you're worried about." But, he thought, I wonder what you expected that little job to be?

"I just don't want you to think—"

"Okay. I don't. You don't go there regular. Does he?"

"How the hell do I know does he go there regular if I don't?"

"All right. All right."

"Look, I don't know nothing about no killing," Eddie said. "That bastard, he told me she died somewheres else, and then I got there with Buck and Tommy and I smelled —hell, I ain't no dummy, I knowed—and then to find out Tommy was a *cop*, I was scared—what call has Tommy got, being a cop?" he asked resentfully.

"He makes a darn good one," Smoky said. "But no, he didn't think you killed her. We did think maybe you knew where the body was."

"You mean you ain't found it?" Eddie asked, looking sick. "God. No, I don't know, it was in a car somewheres is all I know. He tole me he hid it in a car. He said he hid it so good even the buzzards couldn't find it."

"Well, Tommy found it weeks ago. Guess that proves he's smarter than a buzzard, huh? But that morning we were hunting you, all we wanted was to ask you about that."

"And I ain't going to jail?"

"You're going to jail, but not for that. You're going to jail for burglarizing Trinity Finance, and selling Tommy heroin, and grabbing that waitress this morning."

"Oh. Well, I did do that. Is that all? I'm not going to jail for nothing else?"

"Look, Eddie," Smoky said, "don't play games. If you did anything else you know what it is and we'll find it out. So why don't you save us all a lot of trouble and tell me what you're worrying about?"

"Am I in trouble for stomping Tommy?"

"If I had any say in it," Smoky said coldly, "I'd knock your Goddamn head right off your shoulders. But it's between you and Tommy and he says let it alone. So no, you're not in trouble for stomping Tommy."

146

X

WITH A STRONG feeling of frustration they deposited Eddie, under suitable guard, to look through mug books and see whether he could spot the person who'd asked him to move the chifforobe. They sent Linn on to the hospital; after all, Kay had been there since nine the night before.

Simons was now looking at the litter of papers they'd hastily abandoned at his desk the afternoon before. They'd gotten halfway through the city directories and found four names that met the criteria they'd set. None of the four were in Records. "You suppose it's worth finishing this?" he asked.

"I doubt it," Smoky answered, "but I don't seem to have any better ideas."

"Neither do I. Damn, damn, damn! You and I are trying to work four cases at once, do you realize that? And we've got the leads so tangled up we can't tell what goes where. Did you ever try to drive a team of horses? Do you know what happens when you tangle the leads?"

"I never tried to drive a team of horses," Smoky answered, "but I can guess."

"You upset the cart. And I'll bet that's what we're doing."

(Simons knew what he'd rather be doing. His mind kept drifting away from work, back to a small square face surrounded by silver-streaked hair. It was maybe a good thing, he thought, that Tommy didn't know quite how well he knew his mother.)

"What are you thinking about?" Smoky asked curiously, watching his face.

"Huh?"

"Not work, that's for sure. Hey! Snap out of it!"

"Huh? Oh. Okay." He stacked the sheaf of loose papers, stood the three city directories on end, and picked up the four case jackets. He laid the two on Libby Bonner and Cynthia Barnett together on one side of his desk. He laid the two on the abortion murders together on the other side, and then separated them. "We don't really know that for sure." He looked at Smoky. "And where do we go from here? That's all we got, brother, that's all we got."

"All you got on what?"

He looked around, sharply, at Matt Carson, who drifted down early Saturday mornings to see what he could find for the paper, Saturday being the day the usual reporters were finishing up feature stories for the Sunday papers. "All we got on four cases."

"Let's see." Matt walked on in, reached toward the desk.

"Uh-uh," Simons said, slapping his hand down on the folders. "Not for release. Your paper's already done stories on them."

"Freedom of the press?"

"I don't have to give you details of our investigation."

"Is that any way to treat me, when I came over to give you something?"

"So give."

He threw a brown envelope down on the desk. It was addressed to The Editor, *News Messenger.*

Smoky opened it. Inside were copies of the same two clippings he'd seen at Barnett's house. But there was more now. Paperclipped to the news story of the assault on Cynthia Barnett was a note, in the same near-illiterate but clearly disguised hand. "Why was the cat killed? Read the psychological research."

"I think he's overreached himself," Carson said, "when he goes to using that kind of printing and that kind of wording, together. Besides, I remember what Barnett told us in April. But is there any possibility Barnett really pulled these?"

"If you'd asked me that yesterday," Simons answered, "I'd have said, only a very remote one. Today I don't even have to say that much. No. We're sure he didn't."

"I'm glad to hear you say that." Unnoticed, David Barnett had quietly entered the room. "This was in my mail."

It was just a postcard, reading, "I contacted Matt Carson today."

"I didn't think there was any possibility," Carson said. "Because I have one advantage I think neither of you have."

"What's that?"

"I knew Libby Bonner. Not only that. I—" He tapped on the clipping. "I photographed this crime scene. It was kind of a shocker to me. I just had met Libby about a week before, and she wasn't a person you'd forget."

"I didn't realize you were that old," Smoky said.

"Old? I'm not old. I'm sixty. I was eighteen then, but you started to work early in those days, when you could find work. I'd already been a reporter one year. They start most reporters out the same way, in a town this size. They put them on the police beat. Not because it's spectacular but because it's *not* spectacular. It takes a cub to get excited about a burglary—even a robbery, after the first few months. But at the time this happened, they didn't have a police photographer. The one they did have had quit and they hadn't replaced him. So I took the pictures for them when they did have something big, because I was always there with a camera anyway. In those days."

In those days. Now he was the state news reporter and spent lots of his time in Austin. But in those days—maybe he could answer some questions.

"How thorough were those investigating officers, Roy Cassidy and Scott Parker, as far as a crime scene goes?" Smoky asked.

"They were thorough," Carson answered. "They didn't handle it like Jerry Duncan would, of course, but hell, you've got to remember, for all practical purposes they didn't have access to a crime lab. Any scientific stuff had to go to the 'bureau' and most of the time nobody bothered. But they knew their business. If you found a corpse in a chair with a gun in his hand and a bullet in his brain and Cassidy said it was murder, you better not waste time arguing, you better start finding out who did it."

"Do you know if they found any blood in the bedroom?"

"Yeah, I—let me explain. Of course I don't remember all this. But after I got this stuff in the mail, I looked up my notes before I came over here. There was blood in the bedroom kind of beside the door, on the wall. I tried to photograph it but my camera jammed about that time and I didn't get everything I went after. They theorized that whoever the other person bleeding was, he had hidden in there for maybe five minutes—there was about that much blood."

"He hid in there because Davey Barnett came back to get his knife," Smoky said.

"Huh?" Carson grunted, and turned to look at Barnett.

"Not her," Barnett said, "him. Him. I tried to make him stop hitting her. And I still don't know who he was."

"Let me fill you in," Smoky said. "Off the record." Quietly and dispassionately, while the clock ticked off minutes, he told Matt Carson what had been happening.

"You know," Carson said when he was through, "if you weren't a politician, Barnett, I'd have an idea on this."

"What?"

"Print a story that would make him think we swallowed it. That might draw him out into the open, especially if it looked like the police swallowed it too. But it wouldn't do."

"Why not?" Barnett asked.

"It would kill you politically. Retractions never catch up with the story."

"And if nobody catches up with him," Barnett said, "he may kill my wife. Smoky, do you think the idea has merit?"

"It might do some good."

He turned to Carson. "Write it."

"Can't do it. There's laws against libel."

"I'll give you a notarized release. How late can you know for sure whether or not you want to put something in the Sunday paper?"

"Midnight will do, for front page stuff."

"Write your story," Barnett said again. "I'll let you know one way or the other by eleven-thirty."

"It's your grave," Carson said. He got up, leaving the envelope and its contents on the desk. Then he paused. "It doesn't have to be a retraction," he said thoughtfully. "I can make it a banner headline—'Politician On Eve of Election Risks Career To Help Trap Killer'—or something like that."

"Let's catch the killer before we write the story about that," Barnett said.

"Sure thing," Carson answered and vanished down the hall.

"What convinced you?" Barnett asked.

"We never really thought it was you to start with," Simons told him. "We've just been looking at the possibility. But the guy tried to get in your wife's room yesterday. He asked the policewoman if it was Libby Bonner's room. She told him no, but she didn't realize then that it meant any more than a simple mistake. Allowing for the years that have passed, her description matches yours close enough."

Barnett dropped his forehead into the palm of one hand. "Jesus," he said, "somebody needs to help me. Somebody needs to—and I know you guys are doing the best you can. In a way it's a relief, now that I know you

151

know what's really going on, but are those women really adequate as guards?"

"They're as adequate as anybody else," Simons answered. "There's a limit to what he can do inside a hospital, unless he doesn't mind getting caught. And this one doesn't intend to get caught."

"That's true," Barnett said. "He's made that clear."

There was a sudden yelp from the interview room where Eddie was looking at mug shots. Smoky went to check on him. "You find the dude?"

"No," Eddie said, "but I found me. Look here, this here's a picture of me. But I sure don't remember when it was took."

Looking at the picture, Smoky could make a good guess as to why Eddie couldn't remember. With a black eye, a split lip, and a happy grin, Eddie had been feeling no pain. "I'll tell you what," Smoky said. "If you can find the dude that asked you to move the chifforobe, I'll recommend probation to the judge. You understand, I can't make him do it, especially not with the record you've already got, but I'll recommend it. But," he added, "you got to be telling the truth. Because we can tell if it's not. If you just pick out some guy and tell me it's him, I'll charge you with hindering apprehension of a criminal besides everything you already got on you." That charge would not stick for one second, but the threat of it might keep Eddie from getting another bright idea.

"I'll sure try to find him for you," Eddie said, and applied himself industriously to the mug books.

Smoky went out, his hands in his pockets. "Shit," he said, "give me one of those city directories."

They went back to checking names from that big (on paper) area called Autumn Hill.

"North car, you got a signal seven at Fifth and Oak."

"Ten-four," Charles said into the radio. He looked

dolefully over at Tommy, who was driving. "Why is it always us?"

"We must be popular," Tommy answered.

It wasn't, of course, always north car to get a signal 7—a fight or disorderly conduct. In fact, east car was at that very moment out with a signal 7 of its own. It was not a high priority call. Tommy was driving maybe five miles above the speed limit, but there was no need for lights or siren. A signal 7 is usually over before the police arrive, and all that remains to do is check on the condition of the loser and determine whether the winner needs to be jailed or merely talked to.

This one wasn't over.

Tommy knew the address; he knew the house; and he knew most of those involved. There were about ten assorted post-teenagers having what appeared to be a highly heated argument in the front yard. Somebody had a piece of pipe in his hand; somebody—several somebodies—had bicycle chains. And bicycle chains can do damage.

Tommy Inman knew.

They asked for backup units. "On my way to you," west car said, and it was close enough they could hear its siren cut on as they got out of their cruiser.

The combatants heard the siren too. Some of them turned to head for the assorted bikes and cars in the front yard, but Charles was in front of the vehicles, revolver in his left hand and baton in his right. "All of you hold it!" he shouted.

The other car squealed to a halt and two more police came out. Most of the bicycle chains were by now on the ground, as the more sober members of the group put their hands on top of their heads. They knew the routine.

Several, however, had made a concerted dash for the front door, and Tommy and Patrolman Don Hall, considerably curious as to why they were running indoors, went after them. After a minor skirmish they took the three they rounded up and put them outside with the others; the wagon was en route to collect all except the one who had been hit in the face with a bicycle chain. They called EMS—not 10-18—for him.

Tommy and Don went back in the house. "It seems to me," Don said in a puzzled voice, "that there was one more."

They made a cursory search of the house. Then they went back into the living room. "Wasn't there one in a red shirt?" Don asked, looking out the front door. None of the assembled party had on red shirts.

"Uh-huh," Tommy said, and flung open the coat closet door. "Peek-a-boo!" he said.

Walter Ellis looked up from the raincoat he had draped over his shoulders and head. "How'd you know?" he asked sourly.

"Once upon a time I hid from the cops, after a rather animated party, in this self-same closet," Tommy answered cheerfully. "Come on out, it's just a little disorderly conduct charge. . . . Well, well, well!" he said, in unconscious imitation of Smoky. His hands had encountered something in Ellis's pocket he didn't expect to find. "What do we have here?"

"You put a name to it, pig," Ellis said. The closet had been very uncomfortable, and now this wall search position also was very uncomfortable. Being on probation, he had a lot to lose. And furthermore, he felt it was very unfair for Tommy Inman, who knew Ellis's world from the inside, to have turned around and become a cop.

"Well, I think a good name to put to it would be cocaine," Tommy said. "A whole damn lot of cocaine." It was easy to put a name on it; it was still in the bottle in which it had left the factory, and the bottle was clearly labelled "USP Cocaine Hydrochloride One Ounce. Federal Law Prohibits Dispensing Without a Prescription."

"I think I had better warn you—"

"You don't have to warn me a Goddamn thing," Ellis interrupted. "You think I'm gonna let that bastard get away with my money while I go to the slammer for the snow? I got it from Beau Tomberlin. And he's on his way to Houston by plane. He took off an hour ago."

"How nice of you to tell me," Tommy said. It would be a simple matter to have the Houston police meet the plane. "North car to car five?" he said into the walkie-talkie.

After a moment he was answered. "Go ahead, north car."

"Can you twenty-nine me out here?" Meet me, that meant.

"Can you tell me over the radio? I'm kinda ten-six."

Tommy hesitated. This didn't really need to be going out over people's scanners. "Can you walk up to the dispatch office?" he asked. "I'll want to go to tach two and disable."

"Ten-four," Smoky said. "Stand by on two." A minute later he said, "Go ahead." And with the disable switch thrown, no scanner in the city could hear Tommy's excited voice.

"Okay," Smoky said after a moment's thought. "Bring him and it on in. I was wondering where it had gone to." As its loss, belatedly discovered and reported an hour earlier, had coincided with the failure of Beau Tomberlin to report for work, that part of Tommy's report came as no surprise. "I'll get Houston on it," he added.

Ellis was escorted into the detective bureau in handcuffs. Smoky normally would have been elated by the retrieved cocaine, but this time he didn't really feel like taking the trouble to do anything about it. He had too much else on his mind.

But Tommy had worked with him on a day-to-day basis for three weeks after his cover was burned and before he went into uniform. "Tommy," he said, "if your sergeant doesn't mind me borrowing you, will you work this up?

I'm damn busy on this other thing. Here's the key to the narcotics locker.'' He turned his attention back to the old city directory.

Looking at the keys in his hand, Tommy had a very peculiar feeling in the pit of his stomach. Because Farmer's Mound, unlike larger police departments, does not polygraph its prospective employees, Smoky had not known when Tommy Inman was hired that for over a year Tommy had been a heroin addict, only off it a month and a half before taking the job. But he had known it by January, and although Tommy had been trusted with the relatively small amount of money and narcotics he had handled before he went into uniform, he had never before had the keys to the narcotics locker in his hand.

For a person getting over heroin addiction, and not daring because of his situation to ask for psychological help, a year is not a very long time. Tommy knew it. So did Smoky.

"Okay," Tommy said. He put Ellis in an interview room with its closed door in sight of Smoky and Steve and went down the hall. The door that shut the evidence room had three locks. If they weren't opened in the right order, an alarm went off in the dispatch office. The door of the safe that was called the narcotics locker also had three locks and an alarm. The alarm was mechanical, not electric, and any attempt to jump it would set off another alarm.

It was an intricate arrangement for so small a department. It had been devised by a policeman, now retired, who had been some type of electronics technician in the Air Force prior to joining the force.

Tommy knew the order in which to open the six locks. Looking in the safe, he was aware of the odd feeling in the pit of his stomach again. Farmer's Mound is a small town. But it has a large population in the fifteen-to-thirty age group, and it is conveniently close to the Dallas-Fort Worth metroplex, close enough to work dope without being right under the nose of the Metro Intelligence Unit. There must have been a hundred thousand dollars worth of drugs, street value, in that safe.

Tommy put an evidence tag on the still-sealed cocaine bottle. He wrote the tag number in his notebook to put on his report, and logged it in the notebook that was kept inside the safe. One ounce of cocaine hydrochloride, taken from the pocket of Walter Ellis, date, time, address. Mentally he continued. Wholesale value about seventy dollars. Street wholesale value, uncut, four thousand dollars. Street retail value, cut as it probably would have been cut if it had reached the street, eight thousand to fourteen thousand dollars. Tommy locked the safe and took the keys back to Smoky, and he knew, from the absent-minded way Smoky laid the keys on his desk, that Smoky wouldn't be going to check behind him.

What kept that funny feeling in his stomach was that Smoky hadn't made a big deal out of it; he hadn't given him that "now I know I can trust you" speech that really means "I don't know if I can trust you or not." Smoky had trusted him quite casually, just as he would have anyone else he had decided to trust.

In which he was not wrong. But he was wrong that Smoky hadn't thought about it. "I'm worried about him," Smoky said quietly to Simons, after Tommy went back into the interrogation room and closed the door.

"In what way?" Simons asked. "He's damn dependable."

"He's too damn dependable," Smoky answered. "That life he lived for two years—I assume Melissa doesn't know much about it. She doesn't need to. He's ashamed of it. Right now he can't face the fact that one part of his personality is drawn to that kind of life. He'll never return to it, I'm sure of that. But I feel like he's got to learn to accept that part of his personality some way, whether it's by reading *Easyrider* or telling war stories."

"He reads *Easyrider*," Simons answered, "and I've

seen him popping wheelies on that bike of his. But I don't think he ever tells war stories."

There was a burst of laughter from behind the closed door where Tommy was talking with Walter Ellis, and Smoky cocked his head toward it. "Sounds like somebody's telling war stories."

Eddie stuck his head out the door. "I looked through all these books," he said, "and he just ain't in here. Have you got some more books?"

"Sorry, wish we did," Simons answered.

"Did I hear Tommy out here?"

"Yeah," Smoky said. Whatever Eddie had been on had apparently finished wearing off, he thought, because Eddie's eyes were beginning to look tired.

"Can I talk to Tommy?" Eddie asked.

"He's busy."

"Can I wait in here?"

"I guess," Smoky said. It might be just an excuse to keep from going to jail, but he didn't suppose it mattered. Eddie, when sober and not hung over, was not hard to keep track of.

Eddie went back in the interrogation room and shut the door. Smoky guessed he was going in there to sleep.

Tommy came out of the other interview room looking highly pleased about something. He got a typewriter on a rolling typewriter stand and went back in again.

They were almost through checking names. Four more blocks on paper and they would be through. Their list of people who lived in Overlook in 1941, did not live there last year, and did live there this year was up to eleven. After they finished with the list they guessed they would go visit everybody on it. Unless they thought of something better in the meantime.

Very plodding. Very unimaginative. But they had tried everything else they knew to try.

Tommy came back out again, looking even more

pleased. He asked Smoky, "Are you sure it's okay for me to work in here today?"

"I cleared it with your sergeant," Smoky told him.

"Is Charles—"

"Charles picked up one of the walking beats. He's not alone." Tommy, like many police, was very nearly paranoid on the subject of the one-man car. His opinion was not shared by the almost equal number of police who are in favor of one-man cars.

"Okay. I'll be back in a minute." He left with some of the papers he'd brought out of the interview room stuck in his pocket. After a while he came back from the direction of the courthouse and went past the door to the detective bureau, toward the locker room. He came back from there in blue jeans and a green sweatshirt. The shirt was colorfully blazoned with a large red frog which appeared to be drinking Boone's Farm Apple Wine. The frog appeared to be named Jeremiah. At least that was the name on the frog's own sweatshirt, which was blue.

"I'll assume you know what you're doing," Smoky told him, eyeing the frog.

"I do," he said without further explanation and went back into the interview room.

"I think," Simons said, "that my daughter—er—decorated that shirt for him. With something she calls fabric paint."

"God," Smoky said. "It's enough to make me believe in a generation gap."

Tommy came out, this time with Ellis. "You know I'm going to have to handcuff you," he told Ellis.

"Yeah, I know," Ellis said, and put his hands behind his back.

Tommy left with Ellis. He had a radio in his hip pocket, and as he went out the door, he picked up the keys to Smoky's car. He was still looking very pleased about something.

Eddie came back out. "Is Tommy still busy?"

"Yeah," Smoky said. "I'm going to put you in the jail. You can talk to Tommy later."

They took Eddie to jail. Then they went back to lunch, miserably aware that they were not one bit closer to knowing who had committed any of the crimes than they had been at lunch the day before. But they had wound up with a list of twelve names to check.

"There's more where this came from," Ellis told Tommy. "Look, you take enough of it in to make you look good, and I can chalk it off to, uh, public relations. Then you can tell the judge I cooperated with you and he gives me probation, and your boss is happy at you, and we're all okay, right?"

"Uh-huh," Tommy said.

"Because I know you still could go for some of this. This is good stuff."

"Looks like it," Tommy agreed. "Nice and clean. Where'd it come from, out of a hospital?"

"Well," Ellis said, "I don't think—okay, yeah, we got —say a friend. You know? With you to see that it gets through town safe, and letting us know if Ol' Smoky is snooping around, man, we can come out real good."

"Uh-huh," Tommy said.

(But he had talked to Sergeant Jarvis in the locker room. Central car was covering north car's beat, and Charles and Larry Kevane in north car were lying low a block away. Tommy's radio was set on tach 3, and so was Larry's. Tommy's mike was held open by a strong but inconspicuous rubber band. The pocket transmitter Melissa had used would have been even better. But it belonged to the Rangers, and he didn't have time to get it.)

"We've got a shipment comin' in fifteen minutes," Ellis told Tommy. "Actually it's the other half of this one. The dude from Dallas will be here to get it at one o'clock."

"That's close timing," Tommy commented. "It's nearly twelve now."

"It's deliberate," Ellis explained. "We don't want them to see each other, but we don't want to keep any more of it than we have to here for long. Because of Ol' Smoky."

Sergeant Lewis Jarvis stuck his head in the car. He'd been on tach 3, too. "Charles," he said, "I'm going back out on the street. When you get through with this keep in mind tach one will be out all afternoon. They're doing some work on the repeaters, and we'll be operating on tach two. Let me know when that first guy leaves. I'll get him—I already know who he is. You two grab the second before he leaves. Remember, take him outside but before he starts the car. I'll come back and pick him up from you. Be ready to go in when Tommy asks for you."

"Right," Charles said.

All this had been planned, rapidly, by Tommy, who had told Jarvis about it while he was putting on the sweatshirt and jeans. Jarvis had made the arrangements.

And Smoky, Tommy figured, ought to be pleased when he found out about it.

All Smoky had on his mind was the list of names. He and Simons had been able to eliminate six of them by telephone, and they were looking at the seventh when Jarvis came in, somewhat ungently escorting a very peeved-looking young man in a white lab jacket. "That corner interview room empty?" Jarvis asked.

"Yeah, why?"

He scooted the young man into it and shut the door, and put a sack, stapled shut, on the desk. "He's Tommy's prisoner. Don't let him, or this evidence, get away from you. Tommy'll explain when he gets in." He knew Smoky was too preoccupied to open the sack, look in it, and find the two thousand dollars in cash Walter Ellis had just handed over to his supplier. Jarvis was bursting with excitement but he was going to let Tommy tell his own story. Smoky had picked at him often enough about the ineptness of the uniform men on Jarvis's shift (whatever shift Jarvis happened to have at that time), and he was privately delighted to see this somewhat unconventional uniform man stealing a march on Smoky.

"Okay," Smoky said vaguely, and went back to his list.

Desmond Hairston. Resident of Autumn Hill in 1941. Resident of Autumn Hill again now (and resident of Huntsville and several other facilities of the Texas prison system in the meantime, Smoky was well aware). Kenneth Morris. Resident of Autumn Hill in 1941. Resident of Farmer's Mound again. Kevin Varner, Harold Collins, Neil Gibbons, Elbert Cameron, six more names, all residents of Autumn Hill in 1941, residents of Farmer's Mound again now.

A very long shot, that one of them would be the murderer.

Hairston didn't answer his telephone. Probably down at the Black Cat again. Morris's wife answered. Her husband had gone to see about a dog race in Florida—no he wasn't watching a dog race, it was something about getting a dog ready to race—and he wasn't expected back till Monday, and why the police wanted to know was beyond her comprehension. Verner didn't answer his phone. Collins's daughter answered. Her father was in the back yard in the garden and why were the police interested? Gibbons's wife answered. Gibbons had been dead for two months. Scratch one off the list for sure. Cameron didn't answer his phone.

"One of those names sounds familiar," Smoky said absently. He opened the 1941 directory again.

Yes, of course. Kevin Verner lived in the same block as Everett Larsen. It had been Karen Larsen who'd mentioned him as one of the people who'd moved suddenly.

The directory listed him as unemployed. Well, in '41, before the war machinery started moving at the end of the year, a lot of people were unemployed.

Matt Carson came in. "You want to look over this story, Smoke?" he said. "I overwrote hell out of it in hopes I get his attention. And I sure do hate to think of printing it."

Smoky took it, laid it down where Simmons could see it too.

Farmer's Mound Police are today investigating the possibility that the recent assault on the attractive wife of second-term city commissioner David Barnett, who is now running for the legislature, may have been from the same motive that caused the murder of white divorcee Elizabeth Bonner in this city forty-two years ago.

A hunting knife recently discovered and admitted to be the property of Barnett is reportedly being tested by the state crime laboratory for the possibility that it was used in the still-unsolved 1941 killing. Barnett, who is black, admits to being in the room when the murder took place, but is unable to explain the reported presence on the knife of blood matching that of the victim.

Barnett also is unable satisfactorily to explain his whereabouts at the time of the assault on his wife, which police state they "feel sure" was committed by the same person who beat and stabbed Ms. Bonner.

No charges have been filed; however, police reportedly have additional evidence on both cases that they will not at this time divulge to the press, stating only that the 24-hour-a-day armed guard on still-unconscious Cynthia Barnett is "for her protection." Barnett reportedly has asked to have the guard removed.

Police have asked any persons having any knowledge about either of these crimes to come forward."

"Yeah," Smoky said, "I'd hate to see this in the paper too. And yet, I can't see a word in it that is completely untrue."

"The printed word," Matt said, "is a stronger weapon than most people realize. If you know how, you can make the truth more damning than a lie even if the person really didn't do anything wrong. What's this?" He had picked up the list. "Is Kevin Verner back in town?"

"Do you know him?" Simons asked.

"Used to. He was the police photographer back in, oh, nineteen thirty-nine, forty, the early part of forty-one. He quit sometime early in forty-one, I don't remember when —well, it was before July, because I took those pics of Bonner in July."

Karen Larsen had mentioned that. He was a divorced ex-policeman.

Divorced.

Libby Bonner had been divorced, and in 1941, divorce was not as common as it is now.

Some women take their maiden names back when they are divorced.

Smoky stood up. "You may not have to print it," he said. "I'm going over to the county clerk's office."

"Not today you're not," Simons reminded him. "This is Saturday. Anyway, you already know those files are gone."

"Oh, shit," Smoky said, and sat back down again. He reached for his phone. "I'm going to call the chief. His personnel file might still be around here someplace, if the chief will unlock his office. Verner's file might tell his wife's maiden name."

"What the hell do you want to know that for?" Matt asked blankly, and then his eyes widened. "Oh," he said, "yeah, I see."

164

But the chief could not be reached.

"Damn," Smoky said.

"And that's the lot of it," Ellis said, slapping one hand down on the stack of bills. "Pretty good, huh, Tommy? We just keep this little bit of stuff here for local sales, and the rest of it goes to Dallas. We make this twice a week. When's the last time you had a good fix, huh? I knew you'd get tired of that 'straight' gig; I been knowing you too long to figure you'd stay off it. Here's a twenty on account, okay? You gonna get me that coke back, ain't you? On account of it cost me four grand, and I—"

"No, 'fraid I'm not going to get you that cocaine back," Tommy said.

And there was something in his voice—he had stood up, and Ellis, still squatting on the ground in the abandoned warehouse, looked up into the muzzle of a .38. "What the f—Is this a rip-off?"

"Negatory," Tommy answered, "just an arrest for— let's see—several counts of different parts of the drug section of the Texas legal code, and conspiracy, and attempted bribery, and—and—oh, I'll sit down with a district attorney after a while and think what else. Here's your copy of the search warrant. Charles?"

"What the—my name's not Charles."

"Mine is." Charles had opened the door with his foot; he had a .38 in one hand and his baton in the other. "Hi, Tommy," he said. "Larry's outside with the guy from Dallas. You did name vehicles in your search warrant, didn't you?"

It was by no means the biggest drug haul in history. It certainly would not make headlines in Dallas. It might not even make headlines in Farmer's Mound. Street value of it all was maybe twenty thousand dollars, because a lot of it was little stuff. But all in all, it was a very satisfactory haul for Tommy.

Particularly since Ellis was the middleman he'd been trying to get a lead on in April, when his undercover activities had been brought to an abrupt halt.

Ellis, he thought happily, really should have known better.

XI

SMOKY WAS DULY, if absent-mindedly, appreciative of the haul. "How did you sucker him into it?"

"I didn't," Tommy said. "He offered. He did just about all the talking. He was so frantic to get back that cocaine he took complete leave of whatever common sense he might ever have had. I just wish—I wish Charles hadn't heard—" He floundered to a stop, looking unhappily at his best friend.

"I did hear though," Charles said. "Tommy, I knew it already. You don't remember ever meeting me before recruit school, do you?"

"I never did meet you before recruit school."

"Yes, you did. See if you can remember. It was in Dallas. I had on a brown suit, and the guy with me had on a black suit. I knocked on your door and you answered it."

Then memory began to stir. "Oh, yeah," Tommy said.

(A very faint memory. Two young men in suits trying to preach to a group of dopers, talking some kind of nonsense about an angel with a funny name. The dopers laughing, jeering, Tommy catching onto part of what they were saying and laughing, "His angel's a moron, hear him?" The two young men looked at each other and stood up and left, riding away on bicycles.)

"Yeah, I do remember now," Tommy said. "Sorry."

Charles grinned. "You learn not to let stuff like that eat you." He stood up. "You don't need me for the paperwork, do you? I need to get back on the road."

"Tommy," Smoky said, "Eddie wanted to see you. Figure you've got time? If you do, Charles can go fetch him down before going back out."

"Yeah, I got time, but there's no need for Charles—"

"Yes, there is. I need you to tell me some more about Ellis."

Eddie, brought down from the jail, stopped to look at a wall of pictures. "Hey, looka there," he said interestedly. "That guy there in that picture, he looks kinda like that guy I was telling you about. Course he's a lot younger, but his height and that funny way he combs his hair—"

Smoky looked. Eddie was pointing to a group picture captioned "Farmer's Mound Police Department, 1939."

As reporters often do, Matt Carson was sitting in the detective bureau, writing up Tommy's drug raid. When Smoky called to him to look at the picture, he said, "Yeah, that's Verner."

"Do you remember Verner's wife's name?"

"He was divorced," Carson said vaguely, and went back to his story.

Tommy took Eddie back to an interview room. Simons picked up the phone and called the state patrol to ask for a records check on Verner through NCIC. "I'm sorry," the radio operator said, "the computer's down. I'll run it when it goes up, and let you know."

Smoky, on the other phone, had called David Barnett to come look at the picture. Barnett couldn't come. His wife, he explained, was starting to wake up, and the doctor felt it was very important for him to stay there. "Okay," Smoky said. "I just wanted to let you know we have an idea who he might be, if we can find him now."

Then he called Karen Larsen. "Wife?" she said. "Verner's wife? Why, I thought you knew. It was Libby. You know, she took her maiden name back, and then of course she got murdered that awful way just a little while later."

"Thank you," Smoky said. Of course, he thought. It

would have been easy enough for Verner to pick up the phone and call his buddies still on the police force and get details on the case, details such as the name of the colored boy who delivered the groceries. There was still a question about the knife, but right now it didn't seem too important. The only really important question now was, where was Verner?

Smoky tried again to call the phone number he had for Verner. There was still no answer.

Frustrated, he went over to check records, to see if he was maybe on file. He was not.

"Smoky?" Simons had opened the drawer of the small card file that held the fingerprint locator cards. "Look, Smoky."

VERNER, Kevin Roger
W/M 10-3-16   32 II0
                  32 0II

Sec. Guard

Security guard. He'd been fingerprinted as a security guard.

Smoky looked for the fingerprint card, filed alphabetically in the special section where the noncriminal cards are kept. And there it was, the last piece of the puzzle, how Verner got the airport locker key.

Kevin Verner was an airport security guard.

"I'm going after him," Smoky said.

And Simons would have gone too, but just then the radio said, "West car, we have a report of a shooting at 308 Harris."

"I better stand by here till they check on that," Simons said.

And by the time west car could get to 308 Harris and discover the report was a false alarm, Smoky was gone.

*   *   *

"Do you have a Kevin Verner working here?" Smoky asked politely.

The security sergeant looked up from his desk, where he was checking time reports. He was a paunchy greying man, looking maybe older than he was in the grey uniform, and his expression made it clear he didn't appreciate being disturbed on Saturday afternoon. "Who wants to know?"

Smoky produced identification. "I do. Lieutenant O'Donnell, Farmer's Mound PD."

"Oh. Sorry. Yeah, he works here. Why, has he done something?"

"Well, I just need to talk to him," Smoky said noncommittally. "Know where I can find him?"

"He'll be in the locker room. He's s'posed to work eleven to seven but he said he had something come up he had to do and asked if he could swap with Joe, so he'll be changing clothes right now getting ready to come on. Locker's over that way. It says 'Authorized Personnel Only' on the door, but you go right on in."

"Thanks," Smoky said. Swinging the door open he said, "Verner? Smoky O'Donnell, Farmer's Mound Police. I need to talk to you about—"

The man turned. He had on the guard pants and his gunbelt was already on, but the grey guard shirt wasn't buttoned yet, and the vee-neck tee shirt clearly showed the broad white scar at the base of his neck. And Verner saw where Smoky was looking.

Smoky could never remember, later, who drew first, him or Verner—only that suddenly the room was full of smoke and noise and there was a blow that spun Smoky half around, and then a blazing pain so fierce that for a minute he couldn't isolate where it was.

There'd been a snafu. The law requires all security guards to be fingerprinted, and the fingerprints are run through the FBI and the DPS. But Verner's had come

170

back stamped "Not Fully Rolled." Both copies had gone first to the DPS, and normally they would have forwarded the second set to the FBI where a name check would have been run even if the prints weren't classifiable. But this time they hadn't. This time both cards had come back stapled together, just as they went off.

Simons had asked the state patrol station to check him through NCIC, the huge nationwide computer network, as soon as his name was mentioned. But the computer, as per usual when it was most urgently needed, was ten-seven—out of service. Presumably its circuits had been overloaded again. When that happened, the computer would calmly shut itself down to incoming messages until it could catch up.

Five minutes after Smoky left for the airport, with his radio set on tach one, which had been shut down since noon, the answer came back. And the answer was neither short nor sweet.

Kevin Verner was a very dangerous man.

And Smoky's gone after him alone, Simons thought. And he can't shoot worth a damn—because Smoky O'Donnell, that very good cop in most respects, habitually shot in the low seventies, barely enough to qualify quarterly at the pistol range.

"Come on, Jerry," Simons said, and went after him.

They entered the airport building almost at a run, leaving their car blocking the front door. "I'm looking for one of my lieutenants," Simons said, badge case open and in his hand.

"Small, blondish hair, name O'Donnell? Yeah, he went in the locker room. It's right over there—oh my God!"

Because right then they heard what sounded, from a small tiled room, like a minor explosion, rapidly followed by Smoky's voice shouting, very loudly, "Shit!"

There was more in his voice than anger, and Simons went toward the room at a dead run with Jerry Duncan right behind him. Smoky was kneeling on the floor, pistol lying on the floor in front of him, rocking back and forth and holding his left upper arm with his right hand. "Smoky?" Simons said.

"I'm okay," he said, very tightly, "but I think it got the bone. I want to—I want to kick the son of a bitch but it wouldn't do no good, he's dead. Oh *Christ*, that hurts!"

Duncan sat down on the floor beside him. "Let's see, buddy."

Simons went to check on Kevin Verner. There was no doubt whatever that he was dead. A .38 bullet in the head, at close range, does far more damage than might be supposed from its size.

Simons spoke into his radio. "We need an ambulance and the coroner in the airport locker room," he said. "Tell Chuck to head on out here with the camera." Then he set the radio down and picked up the white towel from the sink where Verner had dropped it. Duncan already had Smoky's shirt half off, and Simons wrapped the towel around his arm, asking as he did so, "Where, just as a matter of curiosity, were you aiming?"

"His chest," Smoky said. "I never did shoot very good. Damn it, let go of my hand, would you, Jerry? It doesn't hurt so bad when I'm holding onto it."

"Uh-uh," said Jerry Duncan firmly. "Hands off."

"Is this Verner's locker that's open?" Simons asked.

"Uh-huh," the guard sergeant said, staring at the body.

Simons went over to it. Then he backed off, rinsed the blood off his hands and dried them on a paper towel, and returned to the locker. The top of it contained shaving gear, two more towels, a soap dish. The bar below the shelf had three security guard uniforms, a pair of slacks, and a high-necked sweatshirt. But on the floor was an untidy jumble of papers and scrapbooks and boxes of photographs. Simons opened one scrapbook at random and caught his breath.

"What is it?" Smoky asked sharply. "Let me see."

Simons carried the book in front of him. "Damn!"

Smoky said. "I don't remember one like—turn the page."
Simons turned the page.

Smoky took a deep breath and let it out, raggedly. "So the bastard took pictures! My God, I wonder if we'll ever know how many—it's worth this, it's worth it, to have been the one to stop him. But I would like that ambulance to get here. Because I don't like this."

"Nope," Duncan agreed. "I didn't when it was me." But there was nothing at all to do for the pain, even in the ambulance, until they got him to the hospital and Dr. Hamnet, after checking the situation, ordered a local anesthetic.

"Well, I knew sooner or later you'd walk into one," he told Smoky. "And as if you hadn't already provided me with enough work, I'm told you've got me scheduled for another autopsy."

"Well, at least this is a nice fresh corpse," Smoky said weakly. His stomach was churning but he was determined not to vomit.

"Well, you have done a good job of this," Hamnet said. "How in the hell you expect me—did you feel that?" Smoky had jumped convulsively.

"Hell, yes, I felt that."

"Hold on, then. You'll feel this too, but it ought to finish deadening it."

"Yeah," Smoky said, "only I'm going to—" And he did, into a wastebasket somebody hastily put in front of him. "Oh, damn, oh, damn," he said between gritted teeth, scarcely noticing someone wiping his face. "Hey, don't tell Tommy, would you? Because I didn't throw up because of Verner, it was just because it was hurting so damn bad." He lay back again. "A bullet," he said, "is so damn small."

"Yeah," Simons agreed, "but they hit so damn hard."

"Well," Hamnet said, "I'm not going to try to put a cast on this. Because with the bullet going in through this blasted, filthy sweatshirt you insist on wearing, I'm going

173

to have to watch pretty close for infection. So I'm just going to put a splint on it. And you, my friend, are going to have to take it very damned easy for about the next month. By that I mean you don't drive, you don't work, you don't do anything and if you do she gets on top."

Simons laughed. Smoky didn't laugh. "What about *work*?" he protested.

"You have got, to my definite knowledge," Simons told him, "at least three months' worth of sick leave, seven weeks' worth of vacation, and at least a months' worth of comp time built up. So take some of it."

"All right," Hamnet said a few minutes later. "Smoky, I'm going to let you go home. I'll get you some stuff for pain and some stuff for nausea. You're going to be feeling a little chilly and a little thirsty, but if you go to feeling real cold or extremely thirsty have Audra give me a call. I'd recommend something like hot sweet tea to drink. Don't try to eat anything today, and no booze, it won't mix with the pills. Get you plenty of rest the next few days. I want to see you in my office day after tomorrow. Call me immediately if your temp goes over 101 degrees."

"I don't think I know how to rest," Smoky said.

"Brother, you're forty-three years old," the doctor told him. "I'd recommend you learn, if you want to live to see those kids of yours grow up. This'll help you some, today."

"What's that?" Smoky asked.

"A sedative."

"What kind of sedative? I don't like—"

"It's to calm you down. You've had a hell of a shock. And I'm damn well not going to tell you what it is and have you go looking it up. And don't tell me you don't like shots because everybody doesn't like shots and I'm tired of hearing it. Got me?"

"I guess," Smoky said.

The doctor turned, in the doorway, to look back at Smoky. "I know I can trust you not to overdo the pain

174

pills," he said. "But I hope I can trust you to take them when you need them. You're not going to be doing anybody any good if you don't. And Audra's got enough to do without your causing her trouble."

"Come on," Simons said, detaching himself from the examining table he'd perched on. "Let me take you home."

In the car Smoky said, "Before we go home, let's just go by the station a minute. I need to call Barnett, and I want to look through that scrapbook and see what we can—"

"No," Simons said.

"But I've got to—"

"No," Simons repeated, a little more forcefully. In the large rearview mirror which had been knocked out of adjustment, he could see anger working in Smoky's face.

But then the anger went away. "Okay," Smoky said, in a quite different voice. "Then please take me home."

An hour and a half later, the telephone rang in the old house by the creek. Audra answered it.

"Is Smoky awake?" Simons asked.

"Yes, he's lying on the couch in the living room with Lee watching 'Sesame Street,' " Audra said. "I'll call him."

"I got it," Smoky said. "And I am not watching 'Sesame Street.' I'm watching Lee watch 'Sesame Street.' "

"Just wanted you to know," Simons said, "that we've looked through that bunch of pictures. We've been able to clear up five of ours, from Libby Bonner through Mary Thomas and Rosemary, as well as the assault on Mrs. Barnett. The rest of them we're going to pass on to the FBI and let them try to sort it out, but just in case you're interested, four or five of them are of that Black Dahlia case out in California in the forties. We found a couple of cameras and an enlarger in his apartment. And there was a mighty unusual knife in one of the boxes in his locker. Oh yes, and Barnett says to tell you he's very grateful for all you've done and he's sorry you were hurt."

"Good, I guess," Smoky said.

"And Tommy says can he come see you."

"Tell him tomorrow. No, tell him to come on out. Anything else?"

"Fourteen newspapers and three television stations have called wanting your address. Want me to give it to them?"

"Shit!" Smoky said, and slammed the receiver down.

EPILOGUE

IT WAS TEN o'clock at night, and Tommy, who had gone on four to twelve the beginning of July, was checking businesses on Denton Drive. The back door of the Chopper Shop was open and lights were on. Tommy knew about the agreement with the bikers, but still, it never hurt to check.

Leaving the black and white parked in front, he walked around the side and cautiously looked in the door. Buck Walters was there alone, sweating profusely and trying to do with two hands a job which absolutely calls for four hands.

Wordlessly, Tommy laid the flashlight down and went to his assistance.

Five minutes later Buck sat back on the floor. "There!" he said and looked at Tommy. "Thanks."

"Welcome," Tommy told him. "Glad I happened by." He didn't know how to say what he wanted to say. You don't get sentimental with some people, but he very much wanted to be friends with Buck again. Then suddenly he knew what to say. "Hey, Buck," he said, "I got a problem."

"Yeah?"

"My bike ain't acting right, and I don't got as much time as I'd like to have to take care of it anymore. Can you help me check it, sometime? I got work space in my wife's dad's carport, or I could bring it over here, either one. If—" He swallowed. "If you don't mind helping out a cop, that is. Because I am a cop, Buck."

Buck looked at him, and his face said nothing at all.

Tommy took a deep breath and started to reach for his flashlight. But his hands were oily. He went over to the sink and washed the oil off.

Buck still hadn't spoken.

Tommy retrieved the flashlight and walked toward the door. "Goodbye, Buck," he said, wishing the muscles in his throat hadn't suddenly started aching so. It made it hard to talk.

Buck finally spoke. "When's your day off?"

"Tomorrow and the next day."

"Bring your bike over here tomorrow night. We'll give it a look-see. It's probably that carburetor again. You got a rotten carburetor."

"Yeah. Thanks. Be seeing you, then. I got to hit the road."

He went on toward the car. Eleven P.M. and all's right with the world.

He spoke into the radio. "North car's ten-eight." (Because he'd put himself ten-six at the Chopper Shop.)

"Ten-four, north car. You got a—"

If you have enjoyed this book and would like to receive details of other Walker mystery titles, please write to:

Mystery Editor
Walker and Company
720 Fifth Avenue
New York, NY 10019